THE
GATES
OF SHILOH

THE GATES OF SHILOH

PRAYING MEDIC

INKITY PRESS™

DEDICATION

To Kaylani

ACKNOWLEDGMENTS

I'd like to thank the many friends who have helped in this book's development by encouraging me and providing feedback on the original stories I wrote and posted on social media in 2013. Special thanks to Kimberly Salser, Ginny Wilcox, Todd Adams, David McLain and Elisabeth Cooper. To them, and to all those who supported the concept of this book, I greatly value your experiences, your insights and your encouragement.

I thank Amy Axby, my editor, for her skill, enthusiasm, and patience in working with me on the manuscript.

Thanks also to my wife, Denise, for the layout and production; and Laurie McKenna—a.k.a. Phatpuppy—for the cover art.

1

Bogren moved through the trash-filled alley with purpose, ignoring the men who slumbered among the cardboard boxes, and who, like the boxes, had long been forgotten. Two beings of light stood near a middle-aged man whose shoulder-length silver hair hung over his eyes. Propped up against a cinder-block wall, tears streamed down his face. Bogren surveyed the scene and then drew the attention of one of the light beings. "What are you doing here?" he demanded.

"He is one of ours."

"Are you blind? There's no light in him. He belongs to us." The demon studied the man's face. "You're a loser, Jim. Your father was right. He knew you were a failure. Look at yourself. You've failed at everything you've ever tried. Why prolong the agony? Nothing is ever going to change, and you know it. You were born a loser, and you'll die one."

One of the angels drew near and crouched to look in Jim's eyes. "Don't listen to him. You are loved. Your life has a purpose.

You're not a failure. Don't give up hope. We can help you."

"He's right, Jim. Look at how successful you are. You're on top of the world! Why, everyone loves you, don't they?" He chuckled. "If you had one potential in life, it was to ruin everything you did. And you certainly made the most of it. Tomorrow is only going to be worse than today. More pain. More misery. More failure."

Jim rolled up his sleeve, exposing his forearm. He picked up a syringe and aimed the needle at the vein in the bend of his arm. It pierced the skin. A flash of blood appeared in the hub of the needle. He pushed the plunger. Peace swept over his face, momentarily. Bogren smiled proudly. Jim slid to the ground.

The taller angel grabbed Bogren's arm. "Get away from him!"

"Too late for that," the demon said, pulling his arm free. Jim's spirit sat up from his body and looked around.

"Jim, it's time to leave," said the angel, "we're taking you home."

"You're not taking him anywhere! He's going with me!"

"Bogren," the angel said, smiling, "you always underestimate the power of the light. Look closer. He has it. See for yourself."

The demon moved closer and examined Jim. "I see only darkness. No light. You're lying. Come along, Jim."

"Leave him alone, you filthy wretch! Have you been in the darkness so long that you can't see the light at all?"

The demon looked again and noticed a faint, pink light bathing the outermost part of Jim's spirit. A flaming chariot appeared at the far end of the alley, drawn by horses made of tongues of fire. It moved silently toward them, coming to a stop in front of Bogren. The fiery glow of the horses illuminated the drab walls of the buildings that surrounded them. The angels escorted Jim into the carriage, and, as soon as he was inside, it shot off into the heavens.

Bogren cursed them as he moved toward the other end of the

alley. He passed spirits, both light and dark, that were engaged in battles over other humans, but he ignored them.

He had an appointment to keep.

2

Mocha's sat on the edge of the city of Tempe. Slender palm trees towered overhead, blocking a few warm rays of the Arizona sun. Soon after opening, Mocha's became a haven for college students, morning commuters, and night owls looking for free internet and a good cup of coffee.

Shiloh, a woman in her early thirties with hazelnut skin, stood behind the counter. Jade-green eyes peered out from behind a curtain of long, ebony hair. Distracted from counting snacks for sale near the register, she leaned over a notepad, doodling a sketch of a little girl in a field of flowers. Charity, her manager and friend, passed behind her. "Wow, Shiloh, pretty good for a doodle! Would be great if it had something to do with coffee." Charity laughed.

"Oh, sorry, Charity," Shiloh laughed back and returned to counting stacks of protein bars.

Shiloh and Charity shared a house east of Tempe. After repeated admissions for depression and suicide attempts,

Shiloh had found herself out of work and homeless. Charity offered her a job and a place to stay. Shiloh never expected to work for someone like Charity. She was more than a boss. She was the first real friend she'd ever had.

Near the entrance to Mocha's, where the aroma of freshly ground coffee greeted visitors, a bald man wearing scrubs sat reading a newspaper beneath the sprawling branches of a potted palm tree. A policeman in his thirties held the door open for a tall woman in shades of blue. The woman thanked him, and he followed her inside. A middle-aged woman with blonde highlights sat in a chair near a large window, phone in one hand, a cup of tea in the other. Wisps of steam drifted above a pair of coffee cups at the corner booth where a young couple exchanged flirting glances between sips.

The woman in blue stepped to the counter and studied the menu. "Good morning," Shiloh said. "You look dazzling today! Can I get a drink started for you?"

"Oh, good morning! Thank you!" The woman glanced down at her caftan, moving her hand to arrange the waterfall of silk draped around her body. She wore a ring of raw stone wrapped in gold wire, the kind Shiloh had only seen in museum gift shops. "I'd like a small Americano, to go," she said.

"Hot, or iced?"

"Hot, please."

Shiloh turned to a middle-aged woman stationed at the espresso machine. "Tina, I need a small, hot Americano, to go!"

"You got it, hon!" Tina called back, a bustling barista in a cappuccino-colored apron.

"That'll be two twenty-five. Do you need a receipt?"

"No, thank you." The woman handed Shiloh her credit card. She swiped it and handed it back.

"Tina will have that for you at the other end of the counter in a minute." The woman dropped two dollars in the tip jar.

The policeman stepped forward. "Hi. Can I get a medium, iced, vanilla latte, to go?"

"Of course." Shiloh's sweater didn't quite cover the length of her arms. From time to time, scars on her wrists could be seen. The officer saw them and glanced away. Shiloh tugged on her sleeves. "That'll be three ninety-five. Do you need a receipt?"

"No, thanks."

Shiloh turned to a young, blonde man who wore a perpetual smile. "Tom, I need a medium, iced, vanilla latte, to go!"

"A medium, Robert Van Winkle latte, for the road!"

The man chuckled at the Vanilla Ice reference and handed her a ten-dollar bill. She smiled, made change, and handed it back. He tossed a dollar in the tip jar.

A young man with a crew cut wearing blue jeans and a teal short-sleeved shirt stepped forward. "Good morning, Jack." Shiloh said. "What can I get for you?"

"Large, black coffee, please."

"Room for cream?"

"That would be great."

"Tom, I need a large, black coffee, with room for cream."

"Large, black coffee, with an upstairs apartment for Ginger Baker, Jack Bruce, and Eric Clapton, coming up!"

Shiloh turned her head slowly and stared at Tom. She did her best to keep from laughing, then looked back at Jack. "Major Tom will have that for you in a minute."

"I love this place," Jack said as he walked to the pickup area.

Charity walked past Shiloh on her way to the little office behind the kitchen. "You're doing great today, Shiloh," Charity said quietly, with a smile.

Shiloh smiled back, "Thanks," she said, "I feel good today. Really good." She watched Charity walk away and pondered something she'd said recently. Something about gates. She still wasn't sure she understood. They had been talking about Shiloh's past, her diagnosis, and Shiloh's hopes for a better life.

And then Charity mentioned gates—something about the human soul, trauma, and gates that needed repair.

Charity saw things in the invisible world. For her, life was like one long vision. Shiloh loved listening to her, even though she didn't understand most of what she said. Charity talked about heaven like she had been there. She talked about angels like she knew them. She described things inside Shiloh's mind that were difficult for Shiloh herself to explain, as if Charity could see them with her own eyes.

Shiloh knew of hidden places inside herself where the others lived. Over the years, people had assured her that the world she described was imaginary, but she couldn't believe it was an illusion. It was a very real place with roads, rivers, bridges, homes, and yes, even some old gates. And Charity seemed to think those gates held the key to her happiness. Charity could be a little strange, Shiloh thought. But as strange as she was, no one had ever been as loyal a friend to her. Not even her boyfriend, Frank.

Frank was good-looking and he treated Shiloh well. He was the first man she had let herself think about in a long time. He paid for dinner and let her stay at his place. She'd always had problems with men, but Frank seemed different.

The sound of a motorcycle revving outside turned Shiloh's thoughts away from Frank. She glanced out the glass doors at the entrance where a man in a black helmet and leather jacket rumbled by on a black Harley Davidson.

Gates. Really, Charity? Shiloh shook her head and went back to counting protein bars. The little girl in the sketch on her notepad looked up at her with a peaceful smile. Shiloh started sketching again and watched as a gate appeared behind the field of flowers.

3

Shiloh sat motionless in the lobby of the psychiatric facility. She hadn't been there in months. The orange, plastic chair had a bent leg which made it tilt slightly to the left. Still the same. The only thing different was the girl behind the counter.

Shiloh's hair fell around her shoulders. She allowed a few locks to hang over her face. Her maroon hooded jacket and sweat pants sported a bright-yellow devil holding a pitchfork. It was fall, and football season was in full swing. In Tuscaloosa, the crimson tide rolls. In Tempe, they fear the fork. She peered out at the room from behind a veil of hair. *A bunch of weirdos,* she laughed to herself. And here she was—one of their frequent flyers. A teenager lay passed out on a couch. A middle-aged man paced back and forth, talking to himself. Two older women engaged in an animated conversation near the entrance.

Shiloh had an appointment to see the new intake officer, Emilia Wong. She'd cut herself badly this time. Cutting was a coping mechanism. It was a pain she could control. Visits to mental health units afterward had become routine. She knew what to expect. They would question her, check her meds, scold her a little, and maybe console her, and then release her after a few days. She thought the whole thing was a bit patronizing, but they did what was required by law. That way, whatever she did, they wouldn't be held liable. She just wished she knew why she had done it. Life had been good lately. Charity was great. Her job at Mocha's was great. Frank was great.

The only trigger she could think of was a dream she had the night before. She woke up terrified. In the dream, she was in a dark room with a high-domed ceiling, like a temple. There were no lights. Clusters of candles lit strange patterns around the room. The flames flickered like the eyes of a cat, and suddenly that was all she saw, everywhere, all around her—eyes. Thousands of them, staring, mocking, trapping her. She remembered feeling cold, like she was naked. She felt small, like a little child. Her arms felt like birds' bones—thin, delicate. She hugged herself. A man came out from the dark sea of eyes wearing a priest's robe. He was smiling, but his sagging skin looked dead, gray and waxy. And of all the eyes in the room, his were the only ones she could not see. Where his eyes should have been, there were two black holes. She woke up screaming, looking into those dark, empty sockets.

Later that day, she went into the bathroom and looked at her reflection in the mirror. She closed her eyes to blink, but when she opened them, she had the razor in her hand, and the sink was covered in blood. If she hadn't done it so many times before, she would have fainted. This time, she simply wept and cried out in a weak voice for Charity, who came into the room, gently bandaged her wrist, and silently hugged her the way she'd done many times before.

Emilia's office was a ten-foot square section of the lobby set apart by a temporary wall. A beige partition, four feet high, made up the lower section, and a bank of Plexiglas windows lined the top. Emilia sat at her desk, her eyes fixed on her computer screen. She did her best to ignore the schizophrenic man tapping on the window, trying to get her attention. She had already answered his questions. He would have to wait his turn. She brushed back her long, black hair and rose from her desk. She unlocked and opened the door to the waiting area and walked toward Shiloh.

Seeing Emilia approaching, Shiloh swept her hair away from her pale-green eyes and sat forward abruptly, tracking Emilia's movements. She blinked a couple of times and looked up at the intake worker and then down at her left wrist, which was bandaged, but no longer bleeding. Her dark skin made the white gauze dressing all the more obvious. Shiloh's eyes closed. After a moment, she opened them. Her pupils dilated and then constricted, adjusting to the light in the room.

"Hello, Miss Martinez. My name is Emilia. I'll be doing your intake. I need to ask you a few questions."

"That's fine. But my name's not Miss Martinez. It's Roxanne."

"I'm sorry. I thought your name was Martinez."

"I know. Shiloh—Miss Martinez—she's a sweet gal. But she happens to be busy right now, so you'll have to talk to me."

"Alright… Roxanne. I'd like to do your intake in my office. It's right through this door." Emilia turned and walked to her cubicle. Roxanne followed her and took a seat in the chair beside the tiny desk. After closing and locking the door, Emilia took her seat behind the desk, then began typing on her computer. "So, Miss Martinez, I'm sorry—I mean, Roxanne—are you currently having any thoughts of harming yourself?"

Roxanne smiled and nodded slightly.

"Do you have a plan?"

"Roxanne always has a plan." She leaned her forearms on her knees.

"May I ask what your plan is?"

"You're new here, aren't you?" Roxanne grinned.

Emilia's face flushed. "Yes, I am. Why do you ask?"

"I know most of the intake workers, but I've never seen you before. I would remember you."

"Well. It's only my second week."

"New grad?"

"Yes," Emilia said. She felt herself losing control of the interview. She looked back at the computer.

"You're a fast learner."

"Thanks. Roxanne, can you tell me about your plan to harm yourself?" Emilia spoke in a monotone, all business, resting her fingers on the keyboard, slightly annoyed.

"My plan? I'd like to get my hands on a long, sharp knife… maybe a sword. Then I was thinking I'd kill a few people and then kill myself." Roxanne leaned back and crossed her fingers behind her head. She glanced up at the ceiling for effect but watched Emilia closely while she talked. "Won't get high marks for originality, but I could pick up some style points if I execute it right."

"You're having thoughts of harming others?"

"No, I'm not having thoughts of *harming* others. I'm having thoughts of *killing* others, as slowly and painfully as possible." Roxanne made a slicing motion across her throat with her index finger and smiled at Emilia, showing all her teeth.

"I see. And how long have you had these thoughts?"

"Since the day I was born."

Emilia typed a lengthy note before moving on to the next

question. "Roxanne, do you feel safe where you're living now?"

"Most definitely. Cause I'm the baddest bitch on the block and nobody screws with—"

"Are you currently hearing voices?" Emilia interrupted.

Roxanne snorted. "Hearing voices? That's so rich—isn't everyone?"

"I'll take that as a yes." Emilia looked at the clock. She had another intake to do, and Roxanne was toying with her, wasting time. "May I ask what the voices say?"

"That depends on which ones you listen to."

"And which ones are *you* listening to?"

"Well, personally, I like Becky. She's a great storyteller and funny as hell."

"Becky? Who is Becky?"

"She's like me. Another one of the girls."

"Roxanne, what mental health diagnosis do you, I mean, does Miss Martinez have?"

"Shiloh has multiple personalities. There are some other things too, like anxiety and depression."

"Okay. Thank you." Emilia typed more notes before continuing. "Have you ever tried to harm yourself?" Roxanne pulled up her left shirtsleeve, revealing the bandage and a forearm covered with scars in various stages of healing. Emilia continued typing. "Can you tell me about the last time you tried to harm yourself?"

"I took a swing at a Tempe cop about a month ago."

"That sounds more like an assault than a suicide attempt."

"Things didn't go like I planned. He was supposed to shoot me, but he hit me with his Taser, and I pissed my pants."

Emilia thought the best way to avoid laughing was to quickly move to the next question.

"What about the bandage on your arm?"

"Oh, that," Roxanne rolled her eyes. "Becky does that."

"Are you, I mean, is Shiloh currently using any illegal drugs?"

"Not right now."

"Has she used any in the past?"

"Yeah, heroin mostly. But unlike Sid Vicious, she got off the H."

"Do you drink alcohol?"

"Why? Are you buying?"

"No. I'm not offering you a drink," she said giggling. "I need to know if you, I mean, if Shiloh drinks."

Roxanne leaned forward, emboldened by the laughter. "You're a hot tamale, Emilia. I like your style. If you're single—hell, even if you're not single—I'd be happy to take you out to dinner and show you a good time."

Emilia ignored the comment and made more notes. "Are you currently taking any psych meds?"

"Do you have my bag? There's a list in it you can copy."

"That's great. I'll have security get it."

"Do you have any medication allergies?"

"No."

"Have you ever been sexually abused?"

Roxanne's eyelids fluttered. Her pupils dilated. She scowled. Her face flushed red. She took a few deep breaths, then exhaled slowly. "Yes. Yes, I have," she said, forcing the words out in the calmest possible voice.

4

A small tornado of leaves swirled toward a black wrought iron gate. Bending this way and that, like a drunken man searching for a tavern door, it passed through the metal framework of the gate and deposited the leaves in a mud-choked river. The gate had been fashioned years ago by a skilled craftsman. A dark-haired woman drew near. Timidly brushing aside a handful of spider webs, she peered through an opening in the gate. Frightened little girls ran to and fro being chased by dark spirits. A winged creature circled high above, its body barely visible against the dark, moving sky. It let out a dreadful screech.

The woman took a path to the right and walked along a foul-smelling stream. She approached a building made of dusky purple, green, and blue stones. When she arrived, she went inside and pulled the groaning, weathered door closed behind her.

She stood in the middle of a parlor. A spiral staircase wound its way around the perimeter that had landings at all four of the upper floors. "Ladies, I need to speak to you!" She waited with her hands on her hips. A short, stout woman with red hair walked toward her from the kitchen. A tall woman with blonde hair and brilliant, blue eyes came down the stairs. More women followed behind. They came from all directions. Before long, a dozen women of various ages had gathered around her. "Thank you for coming. We need your help. We're at a mental hospital, and from what we can tell, we're going to be here for at least three days—maybe more, if we don't do something. Roxanne is up right now, but we'll need someone to take over who will cooperate with the staff and play nice until we're released." She looked at the tall, blonde woman. "Jacquelyn, this is your specialty. Would you like to take over for a few days?"

"Why is it always me who has to get us out of trouble?"

The short redhead chimed in. "This is all Roxanne's fault. If that stupid bitch would cool her jets and keep her fat mouth shut, we wouldn't be in this—"

"Lucy," the dark-haired woman interrupted, "I know how you feel, but what's done is done. We can't change it."

"You're one to talk, Lucy, you hypocrite," said a tall woman with auburn hair and green eyes. "At least Roxanne isn't sleeping with every truck driver who springs for a cup of coffee."

"Screw you, Gina," Lucy replied.

"I've really had just about enough of your crap," Gina replied moving closer.

"Stop it!" The dark-haired woman said, "I'm tired of your bickering. Right now, we need someone to go up who will cooperate with the psych facility staff. Unless you want to stay here indefinitely."

"Fine. I'll do it," Jacquelyn said, walking toward the door. "When Roxanne gets back, would you tell her to do something about the darks? They're terrorizing the littles again."

"Thanks, Jacquelyn," the dark-haired woman said, "I'll tell Roxanne as soon as she gets back."

✦ ✦ ✦

Emilia continued typing her report. Roxanne stared at the wall, then closed her eyes. After a moment, they opened again. Their jade green color had become a brilliant blue.

5

A shaft of light fell across Shiloh's face as she slept.

Shiloh held a paintbrush in her right hand and stood, in a long alabaster gown, painting a canvas that hung in the air on a golden cord. She laid down the paintbrush, satisfied with her work. She turned to check her reflection in the full-length, glass window in the church door and brushed a wisp of black hair from her face, then straightened her dress. Her dark skin contrasted with pale-pink lipstick and eye shadow. She felt feminine and beautiful. And whole. A man appeared, ascending the steps outside the church. He opened the outer door and entered the foyer. Like Shiloh, he paused for a moment to check his appearance in the reflection in the window. He groomed his salt and pepper hair with a comb and straightened his tie. He brushed a ball of lint from his tuxedo jacket, then opened the door to the chapel. Shiloh stepped back. The man's dark eyes opened in surprise. "Oh! I'm sorry. I didn't know anyone else was here."

"Looks like it's just the two of us right now," Shiloh replied, "But the others should be here soon."

The man reached out his hand, "I'm Ken. Nice to meet you."

"Nice to meet you. I'm Shiloh," she said, shaking his hand. "I'm sure they're going to have a long, happy marriage."

"They're a match made in heaven."

"Aren't they supposed to be here already?"

"Yeah," Ken looked at his watch, "they're fifteen minutes late. Wonder what the holdup is."

"And none of the bridesmaids or groomsmen are here…"

A bird chirped outside Shiloh's window. She opened her eyes. Daybreak filtered through the opening in the curtains. She threw back the covers, got out of bed, and turned the water on in the shower. Twenty minutes later she was dressed and on her way to the kitchen. Charity was already there, making coffee.

"How did you sleep?" Charity asked.

"Pretty good. Had a weird dream just before I woke up."

"Oh?" Charity's eyes widened. "I love dreams, but some of yours—can you tell me about it? I hope it was better than the last one," she said, handing a coffee mug to Shiloh.

"Yeah. No kidding." She shook a little as she took the coffee mug. The warmth of the mug soothed her nerves and her hands stopped trembling. It was good to be home. "I was standing in a church. It seemed like I was at someone's wedding, and I was painting something on a canvas. I was waiting for the bride and groom to arrive, but they were late. Then a man showed up at the church, and we talked. It wasn't Frank."

Frank and Shiloh had been dating for five months, but Charity had not met him yet. She suspected there was a reason. Maybe Shiloh feared that she would find his weakness. But Shiloh seemed happy with him, so Charity kept her concerns to herself.

"Sounds like a beautiful dream. So glad it was a good one. What else? Did he tell you his name?"

"Umm… Ken. I think he said his name was Ken." Shiloh took a sip of coffee. "We stood there talking about how odd it was that no one was there yet, and then the dream ended."

"Interesting. Have you ever seen this Ken guy before?"

"I don't think so. I'd remember a guy like that."

Charity smiled and took a long sip from her cup. "I had a dream about *you* last night."

"Really?"

"Yes. Really. You died, and I was at your funeral."

"What? Are you serious?" Charity nodded and set her cup down. "I dream I'm at a wedding. And *you* dream you're at my funeral? That's crazy."

"Yes. Your funeral. With some friends. I was telling them how you'd touched the lives of everyone you knew, but I wasn't sad about your death. I had this, I don't know, joy, I guess. I was happy, and they were too."

"I don't get it. Why would people be happy about me dying?" Shiloh tightened her grip on the coffee mug.

Charity ran her hand through her hair. "Well, I know it's weird, especially after what you've been through. But, to me, it symbolizes change. It's like dying to the way you used to live and starting a new life. I usually feel peace when I have a dream where someone I love has died."

Shiloh frowned. This was one of those times. She couldn't accept Charity's interpretation of the dream. She shook her head. *Who in their right mind would see death as the start of a new life?*

Her phone vibrated. She pulled it from her pocket. It was a text from Frank. *Love you, baby. I hope you have a great day!* He was such a good guy. She noticed the time. "We'd better get going."

Shiloh set both coffee cups in the sink, and Charity grabbed her keys. They got in the Jeep, and Charity backed it out onto the road. Shiloh grabbed her fleece jacket and hat from the back seat and pulled them on. "Charity, I'm not saying your dream means what you say it does. But for the sake of argument, let's say that your interpretation is correct. If I *were* going through these changes… what do you think they would look like?"

Charity's blonde hair tossed in the wind. She shouted to be heard over the road noise. "Hard to say exactly. It could be anything from a new job or hobby to a new romance. Might be a move across the country or even starting a family." Shiloh didn't reply. She stared at the palm trees, stucco homes, and fountains as they passed. Thirty minutes later, they arrived at Mocha's. Charity parked in the far back corner of the parking lot, and they went inside.

The warm aroma greeted them, as always. Tom and Tina scooted around the machines and the crowd of customers. When Shiloh walked in, Tom waved a quick "Hey!" and dashed to the espresso machines. Shiloh found an apron and put it on, then went to the register, greeted a woman, and took her order.

The woman walked to the far end of the counter and waited as Tina prepared her latte. A tall man wearing a suit and tie stepped forward. "Sir, what can I get started for you?"

The man placed his order and handed her a ten-dollar bill. She rang him up and handed him the change. He tossed three ones into the tip jar.

"Tom, I need a large chai tea, to go."

"Large tai chi for the man in the suit."

Shiloh rolled her eyes and laughed, then looked at the last customer in line—a man who looked to be in his mid-thirties, with salt-and-pepper hair and ebony eyes. He unzipped his black leather jacket, revealing a Hawaiian shirt. He held a motorcycle helmet, which he placed gently on the counter. "Aloha—"

"Wait. It's you," Shiloh interrupted, "what… what are *you* doing here?"

The man lowered his sunglasses and looked at her for a short moment, then smiled. "*Me?* What are *you* doing here?"

"You were in my dream last night! I mean, umm…" An uncomfortable silence fell over them.

He stared back without speaking. Slowly, he gathered his courage, and finally, he looked at her name tag. "Well, Shiloh… I'm not sure exactly what's happening here, but *you* were in *my* dream last night."

"That's impossible!" she said, placing her hands on her hips. "You weren't dressed the same, but I'd never forget your face. You were painting. We were at a church. Dressed for a wedding. We were waiting for the bride and groom."

"They were late," Shiloh added.

"We were wondering where they were."

"And I wondered where the bridesmaids and groomsmen were," Shiloh said, finishing the dream. "Are you kidding me? You had the same dream? Who are you? No—wait! Don't tell me."

"Maybe I'm the man of your dreams," he said with a grin. "Sorry, couldn't resist."

"Ken!" She blurted out, "Your name is Ken!"

"I told you my name?"

"Yeah. You did." Shiloh's tone became more serious.

They stared at each other.

"Well. Can we talk later?" Ken wanted to say more, but he glanced around, at a loss for words.

"Sure. I guess so. I don't know." Shiloh faltered. "Did you want a coffee or something?"

"Coffee. Right. Yeah, can I get a large, hot mocha?"

"Sure. That'll be four seventy-five. Would you like a receipt?"

"Yes, please… and maybe your phone number?"

"Ken. I should tell you. I would talk to you again. I really would because this is too crazy. But I'm in a relationship."

"Oh. Okay. Well, he's a lucky guy." Ken's smile faded. He pulled a credit card from his wallet and handed it to her. She swiped it and handed it back.

"Tom, I need a large, hot mocha, to go."

"Large mocha, for the Big Kahuna coming right up!"

"Tom will have that for you at the end of the counter," Shiloh said, trying not to stare at him but at the same time, painting a permanent portrait of him in her mind.

Ken dropped a ten-dollar bill in the tip jar and slowly made his way to the far end of the counter. A few minutes later, Tom had his coffee ready. "One large mocha, to go." Ken took the drink and his helmet, and walked to a table.

Shiloh watched him walk away. He was handsome alright. She smoothed her apron and turned to the counter. She tried not to stare at him as she wiped it down. *Mmmhmmm. Oh, girl. A whole new kind of crazy*, she thought. Her eyes flickered and darkened; she shook her head. *Not now, not now. Not switching.* Like the driver of a car, resisting one passenger after another that tried to take control of the steering wheel, Shiloh fought the girls as they tried to come up. From across the room, Ken raised his coffee cup and held her gaze as he took a drink. Flustered, she dropped a towel on the floor. As she bent down to retrieve it, she took her time, and considered staying hidden behind the counter, but Charity called her name. Another customer. When she stood up, Ken was gone.

6

A tall, dark figure stood at the crest of a rocky ridge, gazing over the valley below. Taking in the pink and lavender hues that intensified as the sun drew nearer to the mountains, Drumar, at last broke the silence. "This is my favorite time of day, Bogren. Do you know why?"

"No, sir, I don't."

"It's the beginning of night. The edge of darkness. An end— however brief it might be—to the light that I despise more than anything. Except, of course," he added, "the source of light itself. The end of the day brings me a measure of peace."

"I know what you mean."

"How did things go with Jim? In the alley?"

"We lost him, sir."

"And how did *that* happen?"

"I don't know. I was certain he was ours. I saw no light in him. But they came and took him away after his demise."

"You were able to convince him his life wasn't worth living, but somewhere along the way, he became enlightened, and you didn't notice?"

"I suppose," Bogren said, "that's one way of looking at it. But the light he had was nearly invisible. I didn't see it myself until just before they took him away."

"Well, that *is* a tragedy. But rules are rules. We can torment humans all we want and make their life a living hell, but if they have any light, no matter how small it might be, we have no power to keep them."

"We won the battle, but lost the war."

"I'm afraid so. What's done is done. There are more victims waiting, and I'm confident that you'll have better luck with your next one."

"My next one?"

A window opened between the spiritual world and the physical one. Bogren looked at two women, one with fair skin sitting in an overstuffed chair, one with dark skin lying on the floor, rocking back and forth. Her gaze, vacant. Her lips moved but made no sound.

"Yes," Drumar said, "this one should prove to be a little easier for you. We've been working on her for some time. Her name is Shiloh Martinez."

7

Late Monday afternoon, Charity sat in a chair, cradling a cup of coffee, reading a book. She glanced out the front window at the Superstition Mountains. Elongating shadows of ochre and mauve washed the landscape. Time accelerated. Galaxies spun overhead in a cosmic dance. Meteors rocketed across the sky, leaving trails of amber and gold.

A thought echoed through her mind. *Where's Shiloh?* She looked around and noticed her roommate was not on the couch where she had been a minute ago. She set the coffee cup on a table beside the chair and got up. "Shiloh? Where are you?" There was no answer.

She walked to the couch, then leaned over to inspect the area behind it, and found Shiloh perched on her hands and knees on the floor. Charity wondered if the wedding dream and meeting Ken had been too much for her to process. The last couple of weeks had been unsettling. *What are you doing, Dad?*

Charity knelt down. "Shiloh, can you hear me?"

Bogren sat next to Shiloh on the floor. He whispered in her ear. Shiloh let out a whimper, then turned and crawled in the opposite direction. Charity got up and walked to the other end of the couch. She peeked around the couch and found her friend nervously rocking back and forth on her hands and knees. "Shiloh, can you hear me?"

"Don't hurt me! Don't hurt me!" pleaded the voice of a frightened child. Charity had seen her like this before, but it had been a while. There had been months of progress, always followed by a setback.

"I'm not going to hurt you. You're safe. No one will hurt you," Charity said softly. She hurried to find a blanket in the hallway closet. She walked back, crouched down, and tenderly wrapped the blanket around her friend. "Well, little one, do you have a name?" She rubbed her friend's back gently as Shiloh rocked to a rhythm only she could hear.

"Wendy."

"Hi, Wendy. I'm Charity."

"Don't hurt me!"

"I'm not going let anyone hurt you, Wendy. You're safe."

"What about the darks?"

"Do you see any darks?"

"Not here. By the gate."

"Are they still there?"

"I don't know… I'm afraid to look."

"Wendy, why don't you take a look?"

"Will I be okay?"

"I think so." She thought for a moment. "Wendy, have you ever seen a shining man?"

"Yes. The darks say they're mean."

"Do they?"

"Yes. They say stay away from them."

"Have you ever talked to a shining man?"

"No. They're mean."

"Wendy, do you know where Shiloh is?"

"I think so."

"Can you ask her to come up?"

Shiloh's eyes closed, and then opened. Her face took on a look of confusion, and then anger. She rose up from the floor. Towering over Charity, she looked menacingly down at her. "Shiloh's got nothing to say to you, bitch. Why don't you run along and play with those whore girlfriends of yours?"

Charity stood up and smiled sweetly. "Why, Roxanne, nice to see you again. How are the girls?"

"Oh, they're just fine. And they sure as hell don't need help from you."

"Why don't you tell Shiloh I need to talk to her?"

"Why don't you get lost? You know I don't take orders from sniveling bitches like you." She reached out to grab her, but Charity anticipated her move and ducked under her, quickly moving to a position on the other side of the room.

"Shiloh, come up now!" she yelled.

Shiloh's eyes closed again, and then opened. She looked at Charity. "What's goin' on, girl?" she said with a seductive smile.

"Becky, is that you?"

"It's me, sweet thing." She walked slowly toward Charity. "Why don't we get comfortable here on the couch?"

"Becky, you know I'm not into chicks."

"Now, Charity, don't say that. You've never even given me a chance."

"Look, Becky, I really need to speak to Shiloh. Can you ask her to come up?"

She fell silent. Her pupils dilated. She closed her eyes, and slowly opened them.

Charity sat down next to her. "Are you back?"

Shiloh's eyelids sagged, heavy under her brows. "How... how long was I gone?"

"Only a few minutes."

"Who did you talk to?"

"Roxanne and Becky," she said, laughing. "Oh, Becky. And a little girl named Wendy."

"Wendy?"

"Sweet little girl."

"Have you met her before?"

"Not sure, maybe. You have so many little girls inside of you." Charity patted Shiloh's knee. "If you ever decide you want them to find their home and be healed—"

"I know, I know, the offer is always good," Shiloh said, rubbing the scars on her arm. "I don't think I'm ready yet, but one day soon," her voice trailed off.

"Whenever you're ready, kiddo." Charity returned to her chair and went back to reading her book.

Shiloh resisted Charity's offer and, instead, closed her eyes and waited for the field of flowers to appear—her one place of peace. It didn't take long. A wisp of a girl no more than four, came running through a meadow filled with daisies. She ran until the field turned uphill, and her pace slowed. It was a scene she'd seen many times before, but this time, it was different. The gleaming figure of a man appeared at the crest of the hill. The girl stopped and stared at him. He was pleasant-looking but not especially handsome. He had blue eyes and tan skin. A look of confusion spread across her face. She turned and ran back down the hill.

8

Silence filled the house, except for Charity's room. She talked in her sleep.

Charity keyed the microphone. "Dispatch, this is Medic Three. You can show us staging at 12th Street and Alder. Awaiting further instructions."

"Medic Three, copy staging. PD advises the scene is safe. You are clear to go in."

"Medic Three copies, clear to go in."

Brian drove the ambulance to the intersection at 14th Street and parked behind two police cruisers. Charity got out and grabbed the heart monitor and trauma bag. She met Brian at the back of the ambulance. When the gurney wheels hit the ground, she tossed the gear on the mattress, and they steered it toward the driveway. East of the house, near the street, a teenage boy held his face in his hands. "Hang on a second, Brian." Charity walked toward the teenager. "Where are the police?" He didn't answer, but only sat weeping.

At the far end of the yard, a girl about nine years old sat crying in the grass. Brian shouted to her, "Can you tell us where the police are?" The girl didn't answer. They returned to the gurney and carried it through the front door. Brian grabbed the monitor. Charity grabbed the trauma bag. They quickly looked through the entire house but found it empty. "Where the hell is everyone?" Charity asked. She noticed an open door in front of her and approached it. "The basement."

She took two steps down the stairs. The odor of gunpowder filled her nostrils. With the third step, she could taste it. Looking to her left, she could partially see the body of a teenage girl lying on the floor below. She took a couple more steps and saw two police officers standing silently beside her body. As Charity cleared the final step, she smelled the pungent odor of blood. She looked at the girl and noticed a crimson pool under her head and a revolver lying on the floor.

Brian dropped to his knees and felt for a pulse. The girl's hazy, expressionless eyes looked back at him. Charity connected the EKG leads and powered up the cardiac monitor. "Dammit. You've got to be kidding. She's in a perfect normal sinus rhythm."

"Yeah, but she doesn't have a pulse." Brian started chest compressions.

"What do we know about her?" Charity asked.

The shorter policemen answered, "Her name is Donna. She's seventeen. Her mother is a deputy with the Sheriff's Department. She has a history of depression with previous suicide attempts. She found out yesterday that her boyfriend has HIV. She got a hold of her mother's service revolver, put it in her mouth, and pulled the trigger. The neighbors reported hearing gunfire fifteen or twenty minutes ago. Her mom has been notified. She's going to meet you at St. Mark's Hospital."

Charity inspected the back of the girl's head. Her fingers sifted through pieces of broken bone and blood clots. Lumps of gray matter dotted the carpet between strands of wavy, golden hair. Charity pulled a phone from her pocket and hit speed dial.

"This is Saint Mark's medical control. Do you need to speak to a physician?"

"This is Medic Three. We need to speak to a doctor, please." Charity wedged the phone to her ear with her shoulder and opened the trauma bag, then grabbed an airway and bag valve mask and began artificial respirations.

"Hi, Medic Three. This is Dr. Howard. What have you got?"

"Dr. Howard, we have a seventeen-year-old girl with a self-inflicted gunshot wound to the head. Most of the back of her skull is gone. There's gray matter on the carpet. Estimated blood loss is two liters. She's not breathing. She's in a pulseless normal sinus rhythm. Estimated downtime approximately fifteen to twenty minutes. Requesting orders to terminate resuscitation."

"If she's in a sinus rhythm, you should continue resuscitation."

"I don't think we can move her without leaving most of her brain on the floor, Doctor."

"Look. I know you're in a tough situation here, but you need to do the best you can."

"With all due respect, Doctor, I don't think you want this mess in your ER. I think we should call the medical examiner."

"Continue CPR. Intubate as soon as you can. Give two liters of lactated ringers IV, one milligram of epi every five minutes, and we'll see you when you get here. This is Dr. Howard at St. Mark's clear."

"You son of a bitch!" Charity looked at Brian. "The bastard said we have to transport her and hung up."

"Got any ideas?"

"There's no way in hell she's gonna survive. This is a friggin' joke. Keep doing CPR, I'll intubate her. We'll bandage up the back of her head and transport." She looked at the police officers. "If you guys want to help, you can go out to the medic unit and grab a backboard and the blue c-collar bag that's in the same compartment."

The shorter cop looked at the taller one. "Sounds like a job for you." The taller police officer made his way to the stairs.

Charity pulled the airway roll from the trauma bag and assembled the equipment. She positioned herself beside the head of the dead girl. Her elbows submerged into the gelatinous pool of blood as she inserted the tube into the girl's mouth. "I'm in. Brian, bag her." Charity grabbed a stethoscope from the trauma bag and listened to both sides of the girl's chest. Brian attached the bag valve mask and squeezed it. "Good breath sounds." Charity inflated the balloon for the airway and taped the tube to the girl's cheek.

"Hey Blondie, you mind taking over compressions?"

"Sure thing." Charity took over chest compressions. A minute later, Brian had the first bag of lactated ringers infusing. He removed a pre-filled syringe of epinephrine from its box, connected it to the IV line, and pushed the plunger. "One milligram of epi on board."

He took a roll of gauze and carefully wrapped it around the girl's head, trying to keep the bones, clots, and pieces of brain together. When he was satisfied that the gauze would contain most of the mess, he tore off a length of tape and secured the bandage with it. The police officer came down the stairs and placed a backboard beside the girl's body, then opened the c-collar bag. "What am I looking for?"

"See those orange straps?" Brian said. "Hand me three of them." The officer pulled out three straps and handed them to Brian. He clipped them to the backboard one at a time, then placed the IV bag between the girl's thighs. He disconnected the EKG leads, coiled them up and placed them on her abdomen. "Ready to move her." Brian positioned himself at the girl's head and cradled her broken skull and shoulders in his arms. The cop placed his hands under her torso. Charity placed her hands under her legs. Brian counted, "One, two, three." *They moved her to the backboard and secured her with the straps. Charity continued chest compressions. Brian resumed artificial respirations.*

"We need to take her up the stairs head first." Charity said, looking at the cop. "Since you're the tallest, I want you at the foot end. Brian, you take the head. Try to keep her level or slightly elevated." Charity stopped compressions and bolted up the stairs to prepare the gurney. The two men positioned themselves on the ends of the backboard and carefully made their way up the stairs. They carried the backboard to the gurney, then lowered it. Charity applied the gurney straps. Brian hung the IV bag and reconnected the heart monitor. Charity resumed CPR. The two men rolled the gurney to the ambulance where the red lights flashed, relentlessly.

Charity jolted awake. Sweat soaked her sheets. They hadn't saved her. They couldn't. She closed her eyes and watched as a vision appeared in her mind.

She and Brian rolled the girl's body into the emergency department, as a river of light-pink blood streamed off the back of the gurney. They moved her to the hospital bed. The trauma team continued the resuscitation. Doctor Howard looked at Charity and then at the girl's mother, as he felt for a pulse. He called off the resuscitation. The nurses began crying as they turned and left the room, one by one. Charity glared at Doctor Howard, then turned and stormed out of the room. She walked toward the entrance to the emergency department and kicked the door open as hard as she could, causing it to bang loudly against the wall. She walked to the middle of the parking lot, threw her stethoscope on the ground, and stood there, weeping, bitterly. The vision changed and Charity saw herself, Brian and the hospital staff sitting in a conference room discussing the emotional trauma of the event.

Charity took a slow, deep breath and remembered the days

before Mocha's. The life she had before everything changed. She wasn't cut out to be a paramedic. Coffee was more her speed. At least, that's what she told herself. She flipped on the flashlight that lay on the nightstand, found a blank index card and a pen, and began writing:

Nov 11, Recurring dream. Seventeen-year-old girl with gunshot wound to head. Brian and I respond. Dr. Howard told us to transport. We code her, even though there was no hope for survival. We transport her and cause the hospital to hold its first critical incident stress debriefing.

She turned the light off, rolled onto her back and closed her eyes. She needed sleep. The coffee shop opened early in the morning. *Okay, Dad. That's the third time. What am I missing?*

A question came to her mind. *Why did you go into medicine?*

"I thought I could help people."

Why did you quit?

"I found out that I can't do it. I can't help people like Donna."

Another thought came to her, cutting through the dark like a knife. *Are you certain?*

An image of Shiloh's face appeared, outlined in a bright light.

9

"Any strategies that might be helpful, sir?" Bogren looked to his superior and waited.

Drumar turned toward the setting sun. "Subjects like Shiloh can be persuaded to help us in many ways. She's already had a solid groundwork laid. Some of our best agents tormented her during her youth. She's benefited from a wonderfully tragic childhood. Low self-esteem. No sense of who she is. No clue about her destiny. And no cares at all about religion. With the work that's been done, it shouldn't take much to push her over the edge." Drumar paused, taking in the approaching darkness. "One way to program someone like Shiloh is through repetition of our major doctrines. You're very good at that. Another, is to suggest a course of action by giving her a dream. Or perhaps, the same dream repeatedly. To those who are susceptible to them, recurring dreams are as good as years of hammering into their minds how pitiful they are. And it's less work. But you never know if a subject will comply with a dream until you've tried it."

"Excellent idea, sir. I'd like to get this over with quickly."
Bogren turned to leave and then stopped. He turned to face his
mentor. "Does that make me impatient?"

"Not at all. It could simply be that you desire efficiency. There
are many on our side who would be wise to learn how to do their
work more efficiently. Our people perish for lack of knowledge."

"What type of dream would you suggest?"

"That depends a good deal on what you want to accomplish."

"I'd be tempted to push her toward suicide."

"Then you'll want to analyze her patterns of thinking. Is she
prone to suicidal thoughts? Is she violent? Is she motivated by
self-importance, or does she see herself as insignificant? The
thoughts of most humans are so filled with self-destruction
that most of what you'll find—as you rummage through their
minds—can be used against them. Once you know how she
thinks, you can select the right dream."

"You've given me some good options, sir. Thank you."

"No trouble at all, my friend. But *do* keep me posted on
your progress."

"I'll have a report for you in a couple of days." And with that,
Bogren departed. His dark shape drifted down the side of the
rocky ridge that had fallen into shadows. When he reached the
nearest street, he followed it south toward the city. He desper-
ately wanted rest, but he knew there would be none. It was his
curse, and there was no way to change it. He wandered from one
stucco home to another under the orange glow of streetlights,
until he found the house he had been searching for. He slipped
through the wall and into Shiloh's bedroom.

Bogren stood in the dark of her room among a half-dozen
dark spirits of various kinds. A short, fat demon resembling
an overgrown toad perched on Shiloh's bed. Bogren addressed

a tall, rail-thin spirit that had black saucers for eyes—a Night Seeder. "Greetings, I'm looking for a dream that, hmmm…" Bogren looked at the ceiling as he thought. "Do you have one that involves suicide by a knife?" The demon smiled. Spiders and scorpions crawled in and out of its mouth. The creature reached inside itself and pulled out a dark sphere and handed it to Bogren. "Excellent," he said. Holding the sphere carefully, Bogren leaned over Shiloh as she slept and placed it into her spirit, just behind her eyes. "Pleasant dreams."

Shiloh walked to the living room. It was a sunny day. A thrasher sang in the front yard as it hunted bugs in the Bermuda grass. She turned to her left and glided effortlessly into the kitchen. Pulling a long knife from a drawer, she turned to look out the window into the yard. She held the knife against her ribcage and exhaled slowly. With a swift motion, she plunged it into her chest. Her body drifted slowly toward the floor.

Thoughts gathered in her mind like leaves collecting in a mountain stream. Shiloh sat upright in bed. "Dammit," she whispered. The clock showed three a.m. She got up from the bed and went to the bathroom. Bogren watched from his place near the foot of the bed. She flushed the toilet and returned to bed, then positioned herself on her left side, and pulled the blanket up over her shoulders. A few seconds later, she rolled onto her right side. The green glow of the clock taunted her. She tried to forget the nightmare, but it played over and over in her mind.

Bogren crouched down and looked into her eyes. "Frank doesn't love you, Shiloh. He could never love you. Look at yourself. You're a nut case. A failure. If he did love you, why isn't he here with you? I'll tell you why he isn't here. He found someone better. And that wasn't hard because you're no prize. Who do you think you're fooling? Why not put everyone out of their misery?

The world will be a much better place when you're gone."

Tears welled up in her eyes. She squeezed them shut and a few drops ran down onto her pillow. Bogren whispered words of hopelessness and despair. She rocked slowly back and forth trying to chase the dream and the demon's words from her mind. He stayed beside her the entire night. She tossed and turned until the alarm went off three hours later.

The dawn brought rays of warmth into her bedroom and Charity's usual wake-up call. "Hey, Shiloh, you up yet? Rise and shine. Time to—"

"I'm up," she interrupted. "I'll be out in a minute."

"I'll get the coffee going," Charity said, as she headed toward the kitchen. She got the milk and set it on the counter, then filled the grinder with espresso beans. The grinder whined. She extracted the dark powder and pulled two shots from the machine and tossed them into a tall, thin cup, then began steaming the milk.

Shiloh followed the fragrance to the kitchen, yawning. "Is that for me?"

Charity handed the cup over the counter. "Have any dreams last night?"

"No." Shiloh didn't know why she lied. "Just another boring sleepless night. How about you?"

"I did! I had another dream about you. You were standing in the middle of a park, and this big, blue butterfly landed on your nose. Then I saw the scene close-up. I saw you staring into the eyes of the butterfly as it slowly moved its wings. It was the weirdest thing… it seemed like it was studying you. I watched as you looked at each other until the dream ended."

"You have the craziest dreams." Shiloh smiled. She liked this one. *Why don't I have butterfly dreams?*

"Tell me about it. But I love them. You know, I've noticed something. All the dreams I've had the last few weeks seem to point to one thing… you, my friend, are about to go through some major changes."

"I hope for the better." Shiloh closed her eyes and exhaled slowly. Something about Charity always made her a little more comfortable with the truth. "I did have a dream last night."

"What was it about?"

"I killed myself… again."

"Damn, Shiloh."

"Yeah. I know."

"Why didn't you tell me?"

Shiloh looked out the front window and then into Charity's eyes. "I didn't want you to worry. Sometimes you act more like my mother than my friend."

"Okay. That's fair. Sometimes I do worry. But it's only because—"

"I know, I know. It's because you love me."

Charity didn't respond immediately. Instead, she began making the second shot of espresso for her coffee. She didn't want to ask, but she had to. "Have you been cutting?"

Shiloh looked down at the scars on her arms and rubbed them. "Not lately. Seems like all the cutters are on vacation."

"I can't stand the thought of you ending up in treatment again… or dying." Charity came around the counter and hugged her. "I love you, sis. You're doing so well, and I want you to be happy." She looked at her phone. "We'd better get moving."

Shiloh gathered their things. Charity finished making her latte and went to the garage, climbed behind the wheel of the Jeep, started the engine and zipped out the driveway. Shiloh dashed out the front door and hopped in the passenger side. Charity gunned the engine, screeching off the cement pad, spraying dirt and rocks as the tires dug into the debris-covered road.

"Hold on," Shiloh said laughing. "I don't have my seatbelt on!"

Charity's blonde hair flowed like streamers in the wind as they gained speed. Shiloh always wore a cap inside the Jeep to keep her hair from getting tangled in the wind. She pulled her jacket tighter around her and yelled, "You mind if I turn the heat on? I'm freezing!"

"Go ahead," Charity yelled back, "don't mind me." A black Jeep passed them going in the opposite direction. The driver waved. Charity waved back. The road to the coffee shop cut through the heart of Arizona's farm country. In spring, the morning breeze carries the floral scent of orange blossoms—in summer, alfalfa. In winter, the odor of wood smoke lingers for days. Thirty minutes after the women departed, they arrived at Mocha's.

The shop was abuzz with regulars. Many were on their way to work, but the east valley is also home to thousands of retirees who, after serving humanity in colder climates, migrate south. Charity took an order from a regular named Leo. He always ordered the same thing—an iced, medium cappuccino. "That'll be three-fifty, Leo."

"Here you go," he said, sliding a five-dollar bill across the counter, "keep the change." She returned his smile, then made the change from the cash register and dropped it in the tip jar.

"Tina, I need an iced, medium cappuccino, to go!"

"For Leo, the cool cat-Pacino!" Tom called, grinning over his shoulder as he hurried by.

Leo gave Tom a thumbs up. "That's me." He chuckled and moved to the far end of the counter to wait.

Tina rolled her eyes, "Don't quit your day job," she said, swatting Tom with her towel.

A short, middle-aged woman stepped to the counter. "Hi. I'll have a medium, hot, peppermint, white chocolate mocha."

Charity called, "Shiloh, I need a medium, hot, peppermint, white chocolate mocha, to go." When she didn't respond, Charity went to the espresso machine to check on her. "Hey, Shiloh, you okay?"

"Switching headache," she said, pressing her fingers against her temples, "if it doesn't get better, I don't know if I'll make it through the shift."

"I didn't notice that you'd switched."

"Gina came up," she said, "but only for a few minutes. I always get a headache after she's been up."

"Do you think you can make it a couple more hours? The morning rush will be over then, and I can catch a ride home after work with Tina." Charity began making the mocha.

"Yeah, I can do that. Thanks." Shiloh glanced out at the tables, unconsciously searching the room for a shiny black helmet, her thoughts turning once again to Ken. She wondered if she'd ever see him again. The dream seemed like a lifetime ago. Maybe she'd imagined it. She looked out the window, into the street. Too much to think about. She took a couple of aspirin and tried to clear her mind.

Customers came and went. Shiloh did her best to keep up with the orders. By nine-thirty, the lines had grown short. Charity went back to the espresso machine and put her hand on Shiloh's shoulder. "How are you feeling?"

"Much worse. Why don't you just shoot me and put me out of my misery?"

"The morning rush is over and the afternoon crew is coming in early. Why don't you clock out and go home?"

"Okay, I think I will. Thanks." Shiloh massaged her temples, hugged Charity, and dropped her apron on a pile of towels. She punched out at the time clock and turned to Charity. "I need the keys."

"Oh, right." Charity dug into the front pocket of her jeans. "Here you go," she said, handing them to her. "I'm praying for you, okay?"

"Okay." Shiloh never knew what to say to that. "I need to stop by Frank's. I left something there. I'll see you later. Thanks for everything."

"Get some rest, kiddo. I'll try to be quiet when I get home."

Shiloh turned and went out the back door to the Jeep. She pulled the hat over her head, tucked her hair up inside and started the engine. "Charity," she said to the air, "why can't you drive a Honda like everyone else?" She pulled out onto the road and headed east toward Frank's apartment.

10

Charity was grateful for a business that let her set her own schedule, but the work was demanding. After Shiloh left, she carried the trash bags to a dumpster out back, then gathered up dirty towels and aprons and put them in the washing machine. She ordered supplies, called vendors, and paid the bills. During busy times, she helped Tom and Tina take orders and make drinks. Today, she called the afternoon baristas and asked them to come in early so she could go home to be with Shiloh.

Her pocket vibrated. She pulled out her phone and checked the message. *Can you come home early? I don't know how much more I can take.* Charity typed out a short reply: *Hang in there, sis. Be there soon. Love you.*

Charity returned to the register and felt sadness come over her. Then rejection.

A question came to her mind. *Dad… is that you?*

A faint but familiar voice replied, *Yes, Charity.*

Why sadness? Who's sad?

Shiloh. She needs your help.

Charity took another order, but her thoughts stayed on Shiloh. *Dad... what do you mean she needs help?*

The voice replied. *She's in danger.*

She took the next order. "What can I get started for you?"

"I'd like a small, extra-hot, peppermint mocha. To go, please."

She swiped the man's credit card and handed it back.

Dad... what kind of danger? The room seemed to darken. Sweat broke out on her forehead.

Shiloh is under attack. You know what to do.

Charity's heart pounded. "Tina, can you drive me home? Something's going on with Shiloh. I think it's serious."

Tina paused, looking hard at Charity. "Yes. Of course. Now?"

"Yes, now. Tom, can you handle it by yourself for just a few minutes? The next shift will be here soon. I need to run home."

"I've got it, boss," Tom said, "no problem. You guys go."

Charity and Tina hurried out to the parking lot. Tina held out the car keys. "Charity, you should drive. I don't want to miss a turn or—"

"Thanks," Charity said grabbing the keys as she dashed around to the driver's seat. Her thoughts again turned toward the voice. *Dad... I don't know what's going on. But I need a little help here.*

You know I'll always help you. She waited impatiently at a traffic light. "C'mon, c'mon," she said, tapping her fingers on the wheel. She thought about Shiloh and felt a question arise in her mind that she was afraid to ask.

Dad... am I going to need to be brave today?

She heard him again.

Remember my dear, a teacher is only silent during a test.

11

Shiloh drove toward Mesa and turned on Broadway, then continued for several miles. The Jeep slowed as it approached the apartment complex. Frank's blue Ford truck was parked out front. She pulled up next to it, and shut off the engine. She stuffed her hat in her jacket pocket and checked her hair in the mirror. Satisfied, she slid out of the Jeep and slammed the door. She was excited to see Frank and her headache was lifting a bit. She walked to his apartment, gave a cursory knock, and went inside. "Frank? Are you here?" She walked down the hallway and opened the bedroom door.

A woman scrambled to take cover under the sheet, but Shiloh saw her face just long enough to recognize her friend Gwen. From under the sheet, Gwen screeched, "Oh my God! Frank! What the hell is *she* doing here?"

Frank yelled, "Shiloh! What the—I don't know! I thought she was at work!"

Shiloh's face flushed. Her head throbbed. Her eyes dilated.

"What am I doing here?" Roxanne's voice screeched out of her mouth. "You bastard!" She grabbed a lamp from the dresser by the door, then spun toward Frank and Gwen and threw the lamp as hard as she could. Gwen screamed as the lamp flew over the bed and crashed into the wall. The bulb shattered as Frank yelled, "Get out! Get out! Shiloh! Get out of here!"

Shiloh stepped into the hallway and began running. Her eyes filled with tears, making the parking lot a blur. She flung herself into the Jeep, dug the key from her pocket, and stabbed it into the ignition. She backed out of the parking spot, then threw the Jeep in drive and steered toward the exit, accelerating quickly.

As she drove toward home, self-hatred overtook thoughts of rage and despair. "You're an idiot," she said to herself. "You never learn. Who the hell do you think you're fooling? No one could ever love a screwed-up loser like you."

Bogren sat beside her, picking his teeth with a white sliver of bone. He nodded. "Very good, Shiloh. I'm glad you're finally seeing things my way. You're a real piece of work. I've met some gullible humans in my time, but you take the cake. How is it you never suspected Frank was cheating on you? And with one of your trusted friends. Exactly how stupid are you?"

She replied, as though talking to herself, "I just want one person to love me. Is it wrong to want to be loved?"

"It's not wrong, if you're actually lovable. But you're not. No one could ever love a trashy whore like you."

Shiloh pushed her foot down hard on the accelerator and sped down the street. The cars behind her drifted out of sight in her rear-view mirror. Tears streamed down her cheeks. Her hair whipped in the wind. She didn't dare look in the mirror. She knew what she would see—red, swollen eyes, and a beaten woman sick of her failed, disastrous life.

Tires squealed as she pulled the Jeep onto the parking pad and stomped on the brakes. She bolted for the front door and slammed it behind her. The noise went off in her head like a grenade. She pulled her phone out and sent a text message to Charity, then tossed the phone on the table with the keys. Bogren was right behind her.

"Frank's a real jerk, isn't he? You know he doesn't care about you," the demon shouted in her direction. "He never did, and he never will. No one cares about you. Even your parents hated you."

Bogren had been studying her. He knew her parents had rejected her and that she had been dumped by every boyfriend she'd ever had. "Frank hates you, Shiloh. So does Gwen."

Thinking it was her own mind speaking, she responded. "He used me. He never cared about me. Neither did Gwen. She's a two-faced ass, just like him."

"No one will ever understand you, Shiloh, and you can be damn sure no one will ever love you. Not even God. He had so many great things planned for you. But you failed him, too, like you failed everyone else. The only thing you've ever mastered is failure."

The heaviness in her heart had wearied her, physically. She fell on the bed, sobbing. Then she thought about Charity. Bogren detected her thoughts. "Charity doesn't love you, either. She doesn't even *like* you. She only puts up with you because you help pay the rent."

"No, that's not true," she said. "She's the one person who *does* care."

"Didn't you have a fight with her last week? Didn't she call you a basket case?"

She looked out the window and rolled the thought over in her mind. "That's not what she said."

"You're either confused or incredibly stupid, Shiloh. Charity isn't your friend. She's like Frank and Gwen. Nice to your face, but they all stab you in the back at the first opportunity."

Shiloh stumbled to the kitchen and gazed at the countertops and sink, "What was I looking for?" Her mind was in a fog. Her head pounded. *I should go lie down,* she thought, but instead, she wandered out into the garage. Blood pulsed in her temples. She clutched at her hair. A sharp pain in her left eye felt like a knife plunged inside—a knife, that was it, she was looking for a knife. She pulled a hammer from a toolbox, then returned to the kitchen. Looking at the knife drawer, she stared at the padlock that Charity devised for her safety. She raised the hammer and swung it at the lock, which bounced, mocking her swing. Wood splintered as she smashed it again and again. Finally, the hasp broke, and the lock fell to the floor.

"Damn you, Frank! I hate you! I wish I'd never met you! God, if you're real, why do you let this shit happen to the people you're supposed to love? Everyone says you're a God of love. Is this your idea of love? You're up there on your throne, playing God while we're down here screwing each other over every chance we get! Is this how you run the universe? Is this how you love people? You're a sick joke!"

She threw down the hammer, opened the drawer, and grabbed a long, pointed knife.

12

Charity pressed down on the accelerator. Her heart raced. Her lips became dry.

"Uh, Charity, you might want to slow down a little," Tina said. As the words left her mouth, a blue light flashed in the rearview mirror.

"Oh! No, no, no, not now! Oh, please, Dad, not now!" The police cruiser let out a yelp with its siren. Charity pulled into a gas station. With one hand, she fished in her purse for her driver's license.

Tina found the insurance card and registration in the glove compartment and gave them to her. "It's okay, Charity, we'll get there," she said. A police officer approached the car slowly. Charity rolled down the window.

The policeman leaned down, and in a calm tone said, "Hello ma'am, how are you doing? I'm Deputy Tyler Wallace with the Sheriff's Department. The reason I stopped you is that you were going twenty miles an hour over the speed limit back there."

"Deputy, I'm so sorry," she said, handing the papers and license to him and placing her hands on the steering wheel. Tina sat still in the passenger seat.

Wallace looked at the license and back at Charity. "So, tell me, Miss McBride, what's the big hurry?"

"It's kind of an emergency," Charity replied searching for the right words. "More like a personal crisis. Look, it's hard to explain, sir." Charity felt her heart rate climbing.

Deputy Wallace studied her face. "Why don't you calm down and tell me what your emergency is?"

Charity looked at him. "I don't think you'd understand."

"Oh really? Try me," he replied with a smile.

Charity took a deep breath. "I got a text from my roommate a while ago, and I think she's in trouble. I'm afraid she's going to do something stupid."

"Something stupid? Like what?"

"I don't know," she said nervously.

"Wait here. I'll be right back." Deputy Wallace walked to his car. He ran a check on the vehicle's registration and Charity's driver's license, checking for warrants. Both came back clean, but Charity's name came up as a person of interest. He radioed dispatch and told them he was doing a traffic stop on a woman they were looking for from another incident, and verified her name and date of birth. He walked back to Tina's car, then crouched down so he could get a better look at Charity's face.

"Ma'am, can you look at me for a minute?" Charity turned toward him. He scanned her face. He studied her driver's license once more and slowly smiled. "This is the craziest thing."

"What? What's so crazy?"

"Off the record? You may not believe this, but last night I had a dream, and I think you were in it."

Her heart was still racing, but she laughed at the mention of dreams. *If he only knew,* she thought. "Yes. I know about dreams. Go on."

"I was on patrol, and I did a traffic stop on someone who was speeding. In the dream, the car was this same car. It pulled into this same gas station. I didn't get a good look at her face, but the woman who handed me her license gave me your driver's license. *Charity McBride.* So tell me, Miss McBride, why were you in my dream last night?"

Charity was stunned. She and Tina exchanged glances. She took a deep breath and looked back into his eyes. "Do you believe in God?"

He blinked. "Yes ma'am, I do."

"Me too." Charity replied. *What do I say, Dad?* She continued, "I have a lot of dreams. God shows me things that are going to happen. Dreams, visions, all kinds of things. You wouldn't believe half of them. About fifteen minutes ago, he told me that my roommate was being attacked. And that's why I was speeding. And that's why God gave you that dream. So you would know when you pulled me over that I wasn't just another chick trying to get out of a speeding ticket. Sir, I need your help."

Wallace looked at her, and then at Tina. The women stared back, waiting. "Miss McBride, as crazy as your story is, I believe you, and I want to help you. I really do. But I have a problem. You're wanted for questioning concerning a criminal investigation. The police are at your home right now and they're going to need you to answer some questions."

"A criminal investigation? What? I was at work all day. I wasn't anywhere near my house!"

"Miss McBride, before you say anything else, I need to advise you of your rights. You have the right to remain silent. You have the right to speak with an attorney before answering any questions. If you give up your right to remain silent, anything you say may be used against you in court."

"Are you serious? Am I under arrest?"

"No. There isn't a warrant for your arrest. You're a person of interest. We need you to answer some questions and nothing more. It would be best for everyone if you cooperate with the investigation and come with me."

"Where are you taking me?"

"To your house. That's where you want to go, isn't it? And it helps me, because that's where the people are who need to speak with you."

"Alright, I'll go with you." She turned to her friend. "Tina—" Charity stopped, and Tina grabbed her hand.

"Charity, it'll be okay. Go, and do what you need to do. Call me if you need anything. I'm praying for you and Shiloh."

"Thanks." Charity hugged Tina and stepped out of the car. She walked back to the police cruiser.

"I need to check to make sure you don't have any weapons."

"That's fine," Charity replied. Wallace patted her down. When he was done, she got in the backseat. Wallace closed the door, then climbed in the front seat and informed dispatch he was going to the scene. "Can you tell me what happened?" Charity asked as they drove onto the highway.

"I don't have much information, Miss McBride."

"Charity."

"Right, Charity. What I do know is that your name came up as a person of interest, and I picked you up right after I heard about it."

He drove in silence for the rest of the trip. Charity pointed to her road, "Our place is just up here on the left." They were a quarter of a mile away when she noticed police cars in her driveway. As they neared the house, her mouth dropped open. "What the hell?" Yellow crime scene tape blocked the driveway near the house. The police cruiser pulled up to the tape and came to a stop.

"Sit tight for a second. I'll be right back." He got out of the car and found the Sergeant who was coordinating the investigation. After talking with him for a few minutes, Wallace returned with the Sergeant. The two men got in the front seat and turned to speak with her through the wire mesh grill. "Charity McBride, this is Sergeant Owens."

Sergeant Owens studied Charity before he spoke. "Thank you for your time, Miss McBride. If you're willing to talk, I have a few questions for you."

"Of course. That's why I'm here."

Owens looked at Charity's license and asked some routine questions. Charity craned her neck to see past the crime scene tape as she rattled off her full name, date of birth, phone number and other information without thinking, trying to get a glimpse of Shiloh. She was close, but she could only see the silhouettes of police officers moving through the foyer and beyond. She tried to fix a patient look on her face. Sergeant Owens jotted what seemed like an eternity of notes before coming to the crux of his interrogation.

"So you live at this residence with Shiloh Martinez?"

"Yes. Yes! She's my roommate! Where is she? Is she okay?"

"Please, just answer the questions, ma'am. What is your relationship to Miss Martinez?"

"She's my friend. And we work together at Mocha's coffee shop. I'm her manager." Charity kept her voice even.

"Is she in a romantic relationship?"

"She has a boyfriend."

"Do you know her boyfriend's name?"

"Frank Schmidt. He lives in Mesa. I don't know his address."

"Do you have his phone number?"

"No."

"When was the last time you saw Shiloh?"

"Sometime between nine-thirty and ten o'clock this morning. We were at work. She had a headache and needed to leave early. We carpool, so I let her take my Jeep home. That was the last time I saw her, but she did text me just before I left work, a little after one o'clock. Can you please tell me where she is?"

Owens ignored the question. "She sent you a text? Do you mind if I ask what it said?"

"You can read it if you want." Charity pulled out her phone, found the text, and held it against the cold metal cage that separated the driver and passenger compartments. Owens read the message and jotted more notes.

"Thanks. Do you know if Shiloh and her boyfriend were having any problems? Jealousy, money problems, drugs, alcohol?"

"Nothing that she's ever talked about."

"Miss McBride, to the best of your knowledge, has Shiloh ever been treated for depression or has she ever attempted suicide?"

"Oh, my God. Did she—"

"Miss McBride, just answer the question, please."

"Look, Officer, Shiloh's had a rough life. She has multiple personalities. She's been in and out of mental health treatment since she was a kid. She's tried to commit suicide at least… twenty times."

Owens made another note.

"Please, Sergeant, did Shiloh try to kill herself?"

Owens looked at Wallace, and back at Charity. "We're not

sure, ma'am. Right now we have more questions than answers, but your statements have been helpful."

"Can you please tell me where she is?"

"She's at Chandler Regional Hospital." Owens looked out the side window of the police cruiser. He adjusted his sunglasses, then let out a long sigh. He asked Charity, "Do *you* think she may have tried to kill herself?"

Charity looked nervously at Wallace. As if reading her thoughts, he said, "I think you should tell Sergeant Owens exactly what you told me."

Charity hesitated. "I don't think he'll believe me."

"Charity," Deputy Wallace said, "Life gets a whole lot easier when you separate things into two piles. One pile is called 'My Problem.' The other is called 'Not My Problem.' Right now you have a problem. You're part of an investigation, and you need to tell the truth. That's *your* problem. Whether Sergeant Owens here believes you or not is *his* problem."

"Okay. So. If I'm straight with you guys, will you be straight with me?"

Owens smiled. "I think it's time we put our cards on the table."

"This afternoon, after Shiloh left work, I began sensing feelings of sadness and rejection. I'm not prone to feeling that way myself, and I thought it might have been Dad telling me someone else was feeling that way. So I—"

"Your father told you this?" Owens interrupted.

"Oh, sorry, no... I mean God. So, anyway, I was asking him if the feelings were about someone else, and he said they were—"

"So you talk to God?" Owens interrupted again.

"Yeah. Doesn't everyone? I think it's called prayer."

"Right. I get that. But not everyone has the kind of conversations you're describing, do they?"

"Well, you're right about that, they probably don't. But they *could* if they wanted to."

Owens became silent. Wallace looked at Charity and gave her a nod of approval. He asked Owens, "Mind if I ask a few questions?" Owens didn't respond. "Charity, do you know anyone who might have a grudge against Shiloh? Maybe someone who wants revenge? "

"No one that I can think of."

Owens asked the next question. "Do you have any firearms in the home?"

"Yes. A twelve-gauge shotgun and a nine-millimeter Ruger."

"Thank you. Are they yours?"

"Yes. Shiloh doesn't mind me having them, but she doesn't care for guns. Now, knives are a different story."

"Knives? Does she have some kind of fascination with them?"

"You could call it that," Charity replied. "Shiloh is a cutter. We have rules about keeping scissors and sharp objects in the house. I keep a lock on the knife drawer in the kitchen to keep her safe."

Owens wrote more notes. "Miss McBride, that's all the questions I have for you. We appreciate your cooperation. You're free to go. However, we'll need you to be available for further questions while we finish up the investigation. Do you have plans to leave town this week?"

"No, sir. I'll be around."

"Okay, then. We'll be in touch." Sergeant Owens got out of the car and walked toward his own.

Wallace got out of the car and opened the rear door. Charity stepped out and stretched. She looked at Wallace. "Thank you, Deputy. I've got to get to the hospital, but drop by Mocha's if you ever need a good cup of coffee. First cup's on the house."

"Thanks for the offer. I might take you up on it," Wallace said. "You two are in my prayers."

Charity turned and walked to the front door of the house which stood wide open. Once inside, she met a plainclothes detective whose badge hung from his belt. "This is a crime scene, ma'am—"

"Hey, this is my house, Detective! I had my interview with Sergeant Owens, and he released me. I just need to get my keys." She grabbed them off the table in the foyer. "You have my number if you need me," she said, running out the door toward the Jeep. She started the engine and drove past the crime scene tape that blocked the driveway. She drove across the grass in front of the house and through an adjoining field, then steered toward the road. Once on it, she gunned the engine and drove toward the hospital.

13

"Good work, Bogren. It didn't take you long to get rid of Shiloh." Drumar said, smiling.

The demon looked at his superior, knowing he was being tested. "I'd like to take credit for her demise, sir, but the others did most of the work before I got there. I just happened to be in the right place at the right time."

"That's right, Bogren. Don't ever forget you're part of a team. One may have an exceptional gift. A particularly talented tormentor might rack up an impressive record. But we win and lose together. And now I must ask you what happened to Shiloh?"

"The last time I saw her, she was in the hands of the others who were helping me. Didn't she go with them?"

"It seems that she did not. She never checked in down below."

"She had no light, I'm certain of that. Maybe she's wandering the earth looking for another body to inhabit."

"That's possible. And we do have teams searching for her in the other realms, as well. But since she was assigned to you,

you are ultimately responsible for finding her. And I will hold you accountable if she's lost."

A look of concern came over Bogren's face. "I understand sir."

Drumar turned away from him to take in the moonrise. "Beautiful night. Pity the moon is going to spoil it." Drumar thought aloud. "I wonder if… no… she couldn't have."

"She couldn't have what, sir?"

"There's a slim possibility she was taken above, even though she had not yet become one of them."

"That's never happened to one of *my* humans."

"It doesn't happen often. But I've seen it, in rare cases. Our enemy sometimes takes humans who have no light on a little tour. Sometimes they even visit the dry places. If Miss Martinez is indeed above, she may be there now. I want you to go there and see what you can find out."

"To the dry places, sir?"

"Yes."

"I could use a vacation. I'll leave at once."

"Proceed carefully. Report back to me as soon as possible, whether you find her or not."

14

Charity screeched into the parking lot at the emergency department and slammed into a parking space. From the Jeep, she broke into a full run, weaving through the maze of cars and curbs, across the manicured lawn and gravel rimmed-sidewalks, slowing a little as she yanked the metal handle on the gleaming glass door. Once inside, she jogged toward the registration desk. Out of breath, she spoke to the attendant, "Excuse me? Shiloh Martinez—is she here? I need to see her!"

The attendant glanced at another woman behind the desk. Charity rested her hands on the counter, but her fingers began drumming as she waited. Drops of sweat landed on the mauve countertop. The attendant said brightly, "Can I get your name?"

"Charity McBride."

"Are you related to the patient?"

Desperate to be allowed in, Charity lied, "Yes... uh... I'm her sister."

The woman checked her computer for Shiloh's name. "Okay,

ma'am. I see she's registered. Let me ask her nurse if you can see her." The woman disappeared through a door and reappeared a few minutes later. "Miss McBride, one of the doctors would like to have a word with you."

"Yes, okay, that's fine," Charity said.

"I'll buzz you through the door just to your right. The doctor will meet you on the other side." A buzzer sounded and Charity opened the door. Two men greeted her and motioned her gently toward another open door. The first, a middle-aged man dressed in scrubs and a lab coat with a stethoscope draped around his neck, waited for Charity to sit in an armchair next to a dim lamp, before settling himself on the edge of a low couch, nearby. The other man, tall and thin, in his twenties with black hair, sat easily next to the doctor and looked at him.

The older man spoke. "Hello, I'm Dr. Rubens, head of Trauma Services, and you are—?"

"Hello, I'm Charity McBride."

"Nice to meet you." He swallowed and looked off to the side, measuring his words. "I'm afraid I have some bad news, Miss McBride." His eyes met hers, and he continued, "EMS brought Shiloh in this afternoon. She sustained a knife wound to the neck. The paramedics were able to keep her alive on the way here. However, the knife hit a major blood vessel, and she developed severe bleeding. I want you to know that we did all we could to resuscitate her, but we were unable to stop the bleeding or keep her alive. She passed away shortly after she arrived. The coroner has been notified. I believe the police are conducting an investigation. I'm so sorry, Miss McBride. If you have any questions, I'd be happy to answer them. If you need some time alone, we understand, and we'll do our best to facilitate that."

Charity's mind raced. She wiped her moist hands on her

jeans and willed her body to relax. She had to think. *She's dead? She can't be. It's not her time. Okay, so now you need a plan.* She looked at Doctor Rubens. "I think I would like some time alone with her if that's okay." She tried to think of what to do next and absentmindedly repeated herself. "Yes… I'd like a few minutes alone with her."

"Of course, Miss McBride. We can allow you some time to say good-bye. She's in one of the exam rooms. You're free to go in and be with her. We've removed the IVs and medical devices."

"Thank you, Doctor." *If it's not her time, but she's dead… then you need to bring her back to life.*

"Do you want someone to be with you?"

"No! I mean, no, no, thank you. I can manage on my own."

The three of them stood up in unison. The younger man led Charity through the door. "Follow me, Miss McBride. I'll take you to the room." He led the way past a nurse's station where paramedics chatted with the emergency department staff. Charity followed a few steps behind him. As they approached the room, he paused and said quietly, "This isn't going to be easy. She may not look the way you'd expect. You can spend as much time as you want. If you need me for anything, just hit the red call button on the wall."

"Thanks. I'm sorry. I didn't get your name."

"Salvador, but everyone calls me Sal."

"Thanks, Sal." He gave the door a light push, and it opened. Charity entered the room and cautiously approached the bed where Shiloh's body lay, draped with a clean, white sheet up to her collarbones.

"Oh, Shiloh…" Charity reached out a hand but let it drop. She didn't want to touch her. Not yet.

Shiloh's face looked rigid and pale—not Shiloh, but still

Shiloh—sad, and yet, somehow peaceful. Her waterfall of ebony hair reached halfway to the floor.

Charity stood in the dark room, wishing she had brought someone with her. There hadn't been time. *Okay, Charity,* she thought to herself. *You're here to raise her from the dead.*

Dad, how do I do this? She sensed nothing. *Dad? Are you there?* Still nothing. She drew closer to the bed. "Shiloh! Shiloh! Can you hear me?"

Unknown to Charity, Shiloh's spirit stood in front of her. "Charity? Charity. I'm right here."

"Hang on, sis, don't leave. It's not your time yet!" Charity called to her friend, urging her dead body back to life.

Shiloh looked into Charity's eyes. "I'm not going anywhere." She waved her hand in front of Charity's face. "Charity! Can you hear me?"

Charity gripped her friend's pale, lifeless arms, ignoring their cold weight in her hands. "Get up Shiloh, get up! Wake up! It's not your time!"

Shiloh circled around Charity. Why couldn't she see her? She tried again and again to get her attention, but Charity ignored her. "Charity? What are you talking about? I'm not going anywhere. I'm right here!" She turned to take in the entire scene. It was then that she noticed a pale body lying motionless on the bed. Charity shook the body and spoke urgently to the lifeless figure lying there, in the glow of the room's one light.

Charity released her grip on the body, turned away, and uttered a few words in a strange language. She spoke quietly at first—her words flowing gently and smoothly from her lips. After a few minutes, they became louder and more emphatic, taking on a staccato tempo, punctuated with pauses and quiet groaning sounds.

Unseen by Charity, another figure—one that radiated light— appeared in the corner of the room, holding a large stone jar. The being moved nearer to Shiloh and raised the jar over her body, as Charity, unaware, continued praying. Iridescent blue oil flowed over the sheet covering Shiloh's body and ran onto the floor. Charity paced back and forth, speaking loudly, "You will live and not die! You will walk again in the land of the living. It is not your time to go! I command your body, soul, and spirit to be united!"

Shiloh stood motionless, staring at the lifeless body on the bed. Sal opened the door and poked his head into the room. Charity quickly walked over to him. "Everything okay?" he asked.

"Yes, everything's fine… I was just praying."

"No problem. Just checking," He withdrew his head from the room and let the door gently close.

Shiloh walked in front of Charity. "Sis, I'm really confused. What's going on?" She tried to grab Charity's arm, but her hand grasped nothing, and instead, passed through Charity's body. Shiloh froze.

The light above them bent to form a slender cylinder, funneling upward through the ceiling. A shrieking sound could be heard as a circular field of light gathered in the sky above them. The night itself rolled into a sheet of energy, curling like a tsunami into a narrow tunnel, stretching between heaven and earth. Shiloh levitated from the floor, being drawn upward toward the funnel. She drifted toward the ceiling and tumbled slowly into the tunnel. Once she was inside and moving through the passageway, her body gained velocity.

15

The tunnel took a curve to the left. Shiloh oriented herself so that she could see where she was going. She realized she was not alone.

Shiloh drew back, confused. The luminous being next to her smiled. Almost human in appearance, but larger and brighter, peace radiated from its face. Without speaking, the female figure transmitted a thought to Shiloh's mind. *Shiloh, don't be afraid. My name is Gloriel. I've been with you since the beginning. I'm your helper. I'm here to protect you.*

Shiloh heard her and replied with her own thought. *Where are we going?*

Gloriel answered. *You're on an extraordinary journey. Each of the places you will visit, and the events you'll witness are for your growth. You must remember them as much as you can.*

Shiloh slowly brought her knees to her chest, her own planet, orbiting in space and time, moving faster than the speed of light. She turned her head and glanced at the expanse of the cosmos through the tunnel's transparent walls. Here and there, shafts of colored light appeared in her field of view and receded again. Clusters of stars came into view but quickly passed behind her. A light in front of her caught her attention. Although distant, it seemed to grow closer. As she neared the light, it became a brilliant, golden glow that enveloped her. Just as it reached its greatest intensity, all at once, her motion ceased.

She came to a stop, landing lightly on a floor made of translucent crystal, and, glancing upward, she found herself within a massive coliseum. Its walls were made of the same crystalline material as the floor. The coliseum almost seemed to increase in width and height as she tried to measure its dimensions in her mind.

Looking around, she saw tens of thousands of people. A crowd began to form around her. Some of the faces were familiar. Her aunt, two uncles, her grandmother and other relatives greeted her. She became uncomfortable as she realized she was the focus of their attention.

"We love you," said one uncle.

"Welcome home!" said her grandmother.

Her great-grandmother came forward. "You didn't know me before coming here, my child, but I've known you your whole life. I've been here cheering you on and praying for your success."

Another uncle stepped forward. "You have an incredible gift to give to the world, Shiloh."

Friends she had known came to greet her. Three classmates came to wish her well. These people celebrated her life in a way no one ever had on earth. As the crowd embraced her, sending thoughts of encouragement, love and support, waves of joy went into her body. Gloriel stood behind her, smiling.

"I don't understand," she said. "I'm not a good person. I've done some terrible things. Why are they treating me as if I'm some kind of saint?"

Gloriel nodded. "Shiloh, into each person's life, trouble must come. No one is free of heartache, disappointment, sorrow... or evil. You're no different from the others who are gathered here. You came under the influence of spirits that took advantage of your weakened state. You're here to learn. Now it's time to begin."

Silence fell across the coliseum.

A sphere of energy enveloped her, then slowly lifted her off the floor. All eyes turned toward her. Standing before thousands, yet alone inside the sphere, she began to relive all the events of her life on earth. Every thought, every emotion, and every choice she had ever made played out before her, in plain view of the others—every good, and every terrible thing she'd ever done. With each experience, she felt the emotions of the other person, as well as her own. Each time she was beaten, she felt her pain, but also the anger and pain of the abuser. Every time she was cruel to someone, she felt her hatred and their sorrow. She experienced the times she was molested by her father, her uncle, and strange men and women. She felt the shame from the way they looked at her—their disgust and contempt. She watched as others were brutally tortured beside her in ritual abuse. They died. She lived. Waves of guilt penetrated her heart. She watched herself shoot up with heroin. She watched as she stabbed herself and saw her body collapse on the floor. As she stood in the sphere, reliving each experience, faint rays of blue, purple and amber light began to radiate from her body.

Every part of her private life was open to the crowd, but not one person present had a thought of condemnation or judgment. The others had relived their own lives inside that sphere. They had relived their own mistakes before thousands; no one accused her. When the life review ended, the sphere lowered and opened. She stepped from it, and a cheer went up from the crowd. Waves of love and compassion washed over her. Gloriel stepped forward and took her hand, then ushered her out of the coliseum.

They walked down a beautiful crystalline corridor until they came to a red, translucent curtain of light. "The next part of your journey will take you to a place unlike where we are now. If you're ready, it awaits you on the other side of the wall of light." Gloriel waited.

Shiloh's head reeled from the life review. She looked at the wall of light and could swear she saw a familiar constellation on the other side of it. She looked at Gloriel. "I'm ready."

The angel passed through the beam of light and Shiloh followed. They continued walking in a dimly lit hallway. Shiloh felt the familiar sensation of sand and small pebbles beneath her feet. They walked until they came to a reddish-brown stone door that had an archway carved into its face. Shiloh stood before it in wonder. "Where... where are we going?"

Gloriel made a sound like laughter—a laughter made of bells and rain and breezes and chimes. She stretched out her hand, still laughing, and nodded toward the door.

And it opened.

16

Gloriel passed through the door, blue robes rustling, and started briskly down a sandy path, glancing backwards only once. Shiloh followed her, studying the new world in quiet amazement. The path seemed to have been carved by time and weather out of a waist-high slab of red sandstone. To their right, an amber sand dune rose thousands of feet in height. To its left, was a smaller rust-colored dune. Gloriel walked toward them. As they approached a break between the dunes, a fierce wind swirled into a column, forming a violently twisting tornado of sand and gravel. It bent this way and that, winding its way closer to them. Shiloh covered her face with her hands and ducked behind Gloriel, clinging to her and choking on dust.

Wisps of Gloriel's blonde hair drifted gently before her face as she observed the sandstorm. She glanced at Shiloh with a knowing smile. Turning her attention back to the tornado, she said out loud, "Be still!" Instantly, the sand twister fell harmlessly to the ground.

"How did you do that?" Shiloh asked, coughing and wiping hair and sand from her eyes.

Gloriel's pale eyes twinkled. A smile appeared on her face. "All things are possible, if you believe. You have more than you know. And one day, you'll do things that are far more amazing than this." They continued walking. As they passed the rust-colored dune to their right, on their left, was a shallow ravine that ended at a steep cliff which towered hundreds of feet above a narrow canyon, forming a dry waterfall.

"Gloriel, where are we?"

"The dry places."

"The dry places?" She said hesitantly. Does anyone... does any *thing*... live here?

"Yes," the angel replied, looked intently at Shiloh. "When an evil spirit leaves a human, it comes here, seeking rest."

"Rest?"

"Yes, rest. Isn't that what we're all looking for?"

"I suppose so," she answered.

As she studied the angel's appearance, she felt exposed and embarrassed.

Gloriel sensed her anxiety. "It's okay, Shiloh. You're safe here."

Shiloh nodded. "I know. It's not that. I know I'm safe. And somehow... I know that you love me. There's something else. I don't know how to explain it. I guess Charity would say I'm processing things.

Gloriel laughed again, pure ringing joy. "It's been so long, Shiloh. Too long since we've talked like this."

"We've talked like this... before?"

"Once before. In the throne room, before you came to earth.

"The throne room?"

"We'll take you there, soon. Shiloh, when you were created in the Father's heart, I was there as a witness. He asked if anyone would go with you on your journey to earth, and I volunteered."

"*You* volunteered… to go with *me?*"

"All the angels that are assigned to humans are volunteers. We choose to accept our assignments. I saw your strengths and weaknesses. I saw the gifts the Father had placed inside you. I knew your potential. I knew your destiny and I wanted to be your helper. I was there when you accepted your assignment. When you took your scroll from the Father. We spoke about your destiny before you came to earth, but not since then. Not like this."

"You must be disappointed, then. I failed at pretty much everything I ever tried."

"You haven't failed, my dear. You only fail when you quit trying. One of the decisions you'll have to make is whether you're ready to give up, or whether you'd like to keep going. You're here to learn things that can help you succeed *if* you decide to try again."

They continued walking and came to a natural stone bridge that formed above the deep, dry canyon. As they crossed the bridge, Shiloh thought about Gloriel's choice to be her companion. *Why me?* she wondered.

Gloriel smiled but didn't answer. They crossed the bridge in silence. The angel walked briskly again on a path that opened into a shallow canyon. Shiloh noticed a dark spirit approaching in the distance. She felt rejection and hatred coming from it. She drew near to Gloriel.

"What is that?" she asked.

"An evil spirit," she replied, staring coldly at it, "one you will become painfully familiar with."

"Does it… I mean… does *he* have a name?"

"Yes. His name is Bogren." Gloriel continued walking toward the canyon, its weathered, rust-colored walls rising on either side of them. Shiloh followed close behind.

"The spirit we just saw—are *all* evil spirits like that one?"

"No. There are different types. Each one has unique abilities. That particular one takes advantage of people who suffer from rejection, hopelessness, and self-hatred."

"I don't understand. How does he do that?"

"He speaks to you about the people who have hated and rejected you. He reminds you of your belief that no one will ever love you. You've already embraced rejection, so it doesn't seem foreign to you. Most people listen to spirits like him, believing they're hearing their own thoughts. That's how you become their victim."

Shiloh jerked her head sideways, a line deepening between her eyebrows. "Wait a minute. Are you telling me that... that... *thing* back there was in my head? Interfering with my thoughts? Planting ideas in my mind? That he somehow made me believe I'm unlovable... and that he tricked me into killing myself? That's crazy!"

A man walked toward Shiloh. Gloriel became silent.

"Hello," the man said with a smile.

Shiloh drew closer, her gaze riveted on his. She felt herself falling—falling, into the bluest pool, drowning, dying softly in his eyes, the bluest eyes, *no color on earth is this blue*, she thought, and he held her gaze, and she could not look away, and she saw the world in him. She saw herself, she saw new planets, new life, oceans of life, flowers bursting into bloom, forests covering bare ground, birds dancing in sunlight, raging fires of men and women racing each other to trees hanging heavy with fruit, all this and more she saw in the burning blue of his eyes.

Shiloh blinked, then staggered backward, reeling. He reached out and caught her, and she caught her breath. Gloriel smiled at her, and Shiloh knew peace; she knew it.

"People tell me I have my father's eyes," the man said, as he gently released her. He turned and began walking out of the canyon toward the stone bridge. They heard him call out, "Bogren!" The demon appeared in the distance, then slowly and cautiously drew near, taking his place as far from the blue-eyed man as possible. "Shiloh, I'd like you to meet someone. Shiloh, this is Bogren." He turned to the demon, "Bogren, I believe you already know Shiloh."

The demon's eyes flitted. "What do you want from me?"

"I want you to tell Shiloh where you were today."

The demon's eyes grew wider as he slowly moved closer to her. He stared at her for a moment, surveying her thoughts and then straightened his stance. "Ah, yes, the suicide," he said, proudly. Glancing downward, his attention was drawn to a rock, shaped like the head of a viper, "It seems Drumar was right," he mumbled to himself. He looked again at Shiloh, "You were ready to end your life," he said with a grin, "and I'm always happy to assist you silly humans with your departure. Your death—particularly if it's painful—is such a delightful business."

Shiloh glared at Bogren. "Is he telling the truth?"

"He is. He came to take your life. And I'd like to offer you a new one." He looked at the demon. "We're done here, Bogren. You can leave." The demon quickly retreated into the ravine and disappeared.

The blue-eyed man took Shiloh's face in his hands. She gazed into the brilliant eyes and the blue fire flickering within them.

Compassion rose within her. She thought about the many people she had met during her life who were desperate, in need.

She had never considered helping them. Tears rolled down her cheeks. For the first time in her life, she wished she had done something to ease their pain. She raised her hands and grabbed his, then lowered them from her face. She studied his hands. They were strong and well-worn.

"Who are you?" she asked.

He smiled, then turned and continued walking toward the stone bridge. "Who are you?" she asked a little louder.

He turned toward Shiloh and Gloriel. "Follow me. I'd like to show you something." He turned again and continued walking. Shiloh followed a few steps behind him. They walked over the stone bridge past the sand dunes until they found themselves back at the stone door.

17

The three of them walked down a crystal corridor, stopping in the center of the now empty coliseum. "Shiloh," the blue-eyed man said, "watch closely." He stretched out his hand. Images appeared in front of them in what seemed like a holographic recreation of her life.

"What is this?" Shiloh asked.

"You've seen your past. Now, I'd like you to see your future."

She saw herself standing at the altar of a church, in a wedding dress. Then on a boat, at sea. She saw herself in a delivery suite, giving birth. "What?" she laughed, "I'm going to have a boy?"

"You will," he said, "if you choose to return."

She saw her husband and her son and the days they would spend together. Afternoons playing in the yard. Nights on a tropical beach. Days spent in hospitals. She watched graduations, weddings, and funerals for friends. A car accident. She saw herself learning to walk again. She watched herself struggle through physical therapy. She saw fights with her husband, slamming doors, broken windows, and the days they wouldn't speak to each other.

Her mind filled with doubt, her eyes with tears. "I don't know if I can do this." She gazed at the scene and watched herself as an elderly woman in a nursing home, hobbling in pain, using a walker to get to the bathroom. "Oh, God," she said, weeping. The scene faded from view. The blue-eyed man took her hand.

"Shiloh, I know this is difficult. But before you decide whether you want to return to earth, I'd like to show you something else. Come with me."

He led her across the coliseum, to a corridor opposite the one they had just left. Gloriel followed close behind. As they approached the passage, Shiloh heard the swishing of wings. Gazing upward, she saw hundreds of angels descending, until they circled just above her. The three of them stopped before a door made of finely polished gold. A throne was etched into the door's smooth surface. A look of delight came over the man's face. "Are you ready?" he asked.

"I am."

18

Charity walked slowly across the parking lot she had raced through, hours earlier. She needed to clear her mind; the emergency department brought back too many memories.

Outside the hospital, she walked, sorting through a catalogue of scenes in her mind. She wandered until she stood at the edge of a grassy, green depression ringed with trees—her own private sanctuary, hidden between two parking lots. Loss and anger and the suddenness of her friend's death swept over her. She slumped down at the base of a palm tree, trembling. The dream of Shiloh's funeral replayed in her mind. *How could I have missed such an obvious warning?*

Charity closed her eyes. More images formed in her mind. She heard a sound like a grinding train and cried out as she saw the kitchen, Bogren, and a host of other demons attacking Shiloh, mercilessly. Wielding a sword, a female angel tried to protect Shiloh from the assault. She lunged at the demon, but he fended off each blow with a black shield. She watched as the demon's hands turned into sabers. He took a swipe at the angel, opening a gash on her forehead. Charity wept.

She watched Shiloh break the lock with a hammer. "No, Shiloh," she whispered.

She pulled a knife from the drawer and screamed out her pain at God, and then, with trembling hands, placed the knife against her skin and closed her eyes. As Charity squeezed her eyes shut against the vision, Shiloh plunged the knife into her own neck. With a reflex, a lurch of her body, she jerked the knife and let it fall, dropping to her knees. A stream of blood painted the cabinet doors in crimson, as she fell against the cupboard and then to the floor.

Charity cried out and opened her eyes. She drew a deep breath and exhaled slowly. The sky hung heavy overhead. She swallowed, wiped her eyes and closed them again. She had to see this; she had to know.

The scene continued. She saw a fire truck arrive at her house and a crew work to resuscitate Shiloh. The Lieutenant put an oxygen mask on her while another firefighter checked her vital signs. Everything happened in fast-motion. Charity saw blood bubbling up from a wound in Shiloh's neck. Blood. Blood was everywhere. The Lieutenant held a dressing over the wound. The white gauze turned red under his hands. Charity was suddenly drawn in, deeper. She was there; she stood in the yard and watched the ambulance pull up in front of their house. Two paramedics got out, went quickly into the house and took over the resuscitation. Charity could hear them breathing. She heard every word.

"Let's go. Lieutenant, can you get Chandler Regional on the phone and give them a heads up?"

"Roger that."

"Do we have a name yet?" A firefighter found Shiloh's purse and pulled out her driver's license. "Shiloh Martinez."

The crew loaded her on the gurney and hurried through the front door. Two firefighters pushed the gurney while a paramedic ran his knuckles across her sternum, trying to rouse her. "Hey! Hey! Shiloh! Can you hear me?" He grabbed her left hand. "Shiloh, if you hear me, squeeze my hand."

They loaded the gurney into the ambulance and climbed in. One firefighter prepped an IV, while a paramedic put a tourniquet on Shiloh's arm. Another firefighter stacked dressings, one by one, on her neck. As quickly as he added a new one, it soaked through with blood which dripped onto the floor.

The lead paramedic yelled to the driver, "Let's get rolling, a nice, easy code three, please." The paramedic stared at Shiloh's forearms which were covered with scars. "Guys, not that it matters, but didn't we transport her a couple months ago? I know I've seen these scars before."

A firefighter glanced at her arms. "Yup. She's a frequent flyer. Hey, your IV's ready." The medic got the IV started. As they rounded a corner, a river of red flowed toward the side door of the ambulance.

A few minutes later, the ambulance rolled to a stop at the hospital. The men jumped out and unloaded the gurney, then wheeled it inside. As they approached the nurse's station, a man in blue scrubs asked, "Is this the stabbing?"

"Yeah," the younger paramedic said.

"We have you in trauma room two. The team is waiting." They wheeled the gurney toward the room and quickly moved her to the exam table.

"I'm ready for your report," the Doctor said, as he pulled on gloves and leaned over Shiloh.

"We have a thirty-three-year-old female with a knife wound to the right anterior neck with uncontrolled bleeding. Time of the incident, as far as we can tell, was about twenty-five minutes ago. She was unresponsive when we arrived. No family or relatives on scene, and no one has been notified. By the scars on her arms, I'm guessing she's a cutter with prior suicide attempts."

The doctor nodded. "Someone check for a pulse."

A nurse reached in. "No pulse."

"Okay, start CPR. I want head, neck and chest x-rays, trauma labs, hang some O-negative blood, and give epinephrine every five minutes. Intubate as soon as possible." The team worked on Shiloh for another half hour, but she never regained a pulse.

Charity continued watching the scene, in her mind. She watched as they disconnected IV lines and moved Shiloh to another room. They placed a clean, white sheet over her, adjusted the lights, and left her alone on the table. Charity saw herself arrive and begin praying, declaring life over her friend. She saw the angel appear and pour oil over Shiloh, as she pleaded for her best friend's life. She watched herself leave the room, in tears.

She opened her eyes, took a deep breath, and closed them once more.

As she continued watching, two attendants came into the room. They lifted Shiloh's limp body into a white bag, zipped it shut, and transferred it to a stainless-steel cart. They wheeled her body to an elevator. The elevator took them down one floor and the door opened. The wheels clicked against the floor as the men rolled the cart down the hall and into the morgue. Cold air met them as one attendant unlocked the door and the other pushed the cart inside the room. The body bag settled, heavy, into a cooler as the lid dropped shut, metal echoing against metal in the gray light.

19

Under the dim glow of a forty-watt bulb, Shiloh's boyfriend, Frank, sat at a tiny kitchen table, pondering the meaninglessness of life. Gwen lay unconscious on the floor behind him. He took a long drag from the cigarette that dangled from his fingers. Standing behind him, unnoticed, a dark spirit surveyed his thoughts.

"Love?" the demon said laughing, "she never even *liked* you. All she wanted was your money." Frank considered the spirit's words and took another drag.

What an idiot. How could I let her use me?

The spirit moved in front of Frank and stared into his eyes, studying his thoughts. "You're right, Frank. You *are* an idiot. And now you don't have either one. Shiloh's dead, and Gwen dumped you. Why don't you just admit it? You're nothing but a loser."

He picked up the magazine for his Glock and began loading it with bullets. When it would take no more, he shoved the magazine into the receiver and laid the gun back down on the table, then took another drag from the cigarette.

"I don't know much, Frank," the demon said, "but I *do* know a loser when I see one, and you are a model for all humanity to follow. Your stupidity may win you entrance in the fool's hall of fame."

Frank glanced at Gwen's body on the floor. He looked back at the Glock, then picked it up and pointed it at his forehead. "Now you're making sense," Bogren whispered to him. "Go ahead. Make my day."

20

Shiloh, Gloriel, and the blue-eyed man stood before the golden door. The man stretched out his hand and the door flashed as it swung open, beckoning them to enter.

Gloriel looked at Shiloh with wide eyes, and the three of them walked into the dark, cavernous room. The angels that had been circling above, glided through the open passage. An African elephant, illuminated in a soft light, caught Shiloh's attention. It trumpeted frantically and flapped its ears. She drew near to it, in wonder. Standing before the pachyderm, she glanced back at the blue-eyed man, expecting an explanation, but there was none. He smiled, then pointed behind her.

Another light shone on a massive golden seat, occupied by a benevolent-looking old man. He smiled and motioned for her to come closer. As she approached, she felt in her spirit, a sense of safety. "Hello, my dear," the old man said, his fiery blue eyes twinkling. "Welcome home."

Without warning, a woman appeared, lying on the floor

_ront of them. Illuminated in a beam of light, she cried and sobbed before the old man.

"Help me! Someone please help me!"

Her clothing was torn, and her body was covered in deep bruises. Shiloh knelt down and stared at her. The woman did not appear to see her. She continued begging for help.

"I know her!" Shiloh said.

The old man looked at her. "Do you?"

"It's Gwen. She's my friend. At least she was, until I caught her with Frank."

"What do you think we should do with her?" the old man asked. Shiloh glanced again at the elephant, which trumpeted even louder. She looked up and noticed the angels circling above her. They seemed to be laughing. The old man motioned again for her to come closer.

Gwen begged for help, the elephant roared, and the angels laughed, but all Shiloh knew was peace. The old man stood near to her—fatherly, safe.

The old man asked Gwen to stand and then motioned for her to come near. Shiloh noticed a slender thread coming from her own belly. She tugged on it and realized it was connected to Gwen's body. She looked at the old man.

"What's this?" she asked, holding the string in her hand.

He looked into her eyes and again asked, "What do you think we should do with her?"

As she stood beside him, a sense of mercy slowly came over her. Like a thick coating of honey, starting at her head, it dripped down slowly, over her shoulders and back until it covered her entire body. She turned to the elephant which had become silent. Making eye contact with the pachyderm, she could swear she saw it wink at her.

"Forgive her," Shiloh said, turning back to the old man. "I forgive her. Please, let her go."

"Are you certain?"

"Yes. She doesn't know any better. I forgive her. We have to let her go."

"Shiloh," he said to her thoughtfully, "if you choose to forgive anyone's sins, they are forgiven. And you are both free. But if you choose to hold anyone's sins against them, they remain—and you remain bound to them." Shiloh looked down and noticed that the cord which had connected them was gone. "Forgiveness is as much for your sake as for hers," he said. "Bring her clean clothes!"

Two angels descended into the light. One had a wash basin and towel. The other held a long, white robe in one hand. The first angel cleaned the blood from her and dried her skin. The second helped her into the robe. The old man motioned for Gwen to come closer.

"No!" Shiloh shouted.

The old man looked at Shiloh, "No?"

"No. I don't feel like sharing you with her." Shiloh gazed into the old man's eyes, and heard the word *forgiveness*. "Okay, let her," she said reluctantly.

The old man motioned again for Gwen to draw near. She looked at herself in amazement as she approached the throne. She climbed onto it and sat beside the old man. He smiled, then held Gwen in a long embrace. She drifted off to sleep. A moment later, she disappeared.

Another spotlight illuminated a man, sitting at a small table. A cigarette dangled from one hand. He held a pistol in the other. He dropped the cigarette and held the gun to his face with both hands. Shiloh saw a spirit standing beside him, speaking to him.

"Stop him!" she shouted. "We have to stop him!" She looked

..1e old man, who said nothing. "Frank, don't do it!" she yelled as she jumped up and ran toward him. As she did, she saw a black cord coming from her that connected her to Frank.

"I forgive you, I forgive you, I forgive you!" she said weeping. "Don't pull the trigger, Frank." She turned to the demon, "Leave him alone!"

"Shiloh, come and sit with me." Puzzled at his request, she slowly walked toward him. She stood before the golden seat, then climbed to the throne where Gwen sat moments before.

"What shall we do with Frank?"

Shiloh took a deep breath. She sighed. "Set him free."

Her stomach warmed with mercy, and the heat spread throughout her body, filling her with a sense of injustice as the demon taunted Frank.

"That thing—it's going to kill him!" she said angrily. "Demon, be gone, now!" The demon instantly vanished. She jumped down from the old man's side and walked toward Frank, who had risen from his seat. She placed her hands on his shoulders and looked into his unseeing eyes. "Frank," she said, "I release you from the anger I've held against you. I'm sorry for any pain I caused you. I want you to be free to live your life the way you were intended to live it. I love you, Frank, and I forgive you." The image faded, and Shiloh returned to the old man, then climbed once more into the throne, beside him.

"Forgiveness," she said.

"Yes, Shiloh. Forgiveness."

"Why did I have to sit here with you to make the demon go away?"

"Shiloh, I created this seat in a special way. It's a seat of *authority*." He paused for a moment to let the words sink in. "A seat of authority grants special privilege to the one who sits on it.

It empowers them. Whenever anyone occupies a seat of authority, the thing they decree must come to pass. When you sat on my seat of authority, the demon was removed, just as you said."

Another scene appeared in front of them. A man was lying in a hospital bed, surrounded by a team of doctors and nurses that frantically tried to resuscitate him. One of them was performing CPR.

"Do I know him?" Shiloh asked.

"Yes."

Shiloh got up and stepped closer to see who it was. "It's my uncle Paul!"

She noticed a spirit with its hands clutching Paul's throat. Anger rose up inside of her.

"Let go of him!" she yelled at the demon.

"Shiloh, what are you going to do from there?"

She thought for a moment, then ran over to the golden chair, and sat back down. "Evil spirit, be gone, this instant!"

She looked again, and the spirit had vanished, but the medical team continued the resuscitation.

"I don't understand," Shiloh said.

"Would you like more information?"

"Yes!" The hospital scene remained, but another scene appeared beside it. Shiloh looked at the screen of a medical imaging device that displayed a glowing strand of DNA. One section of the strand was highlighted in purple. What's that?" she asked.

"Why don't you have a closer look?"

She drew nearer and scrutinized the strand of DNA, noting its regular patterns, and then, she noticed an irregularity. She walked back to the seat and sat down. Indignation rose up in her spirit, making her emboldened and more determined. "DNA,

.nmand you to become normal!" She looked again at the
ᴗNA. The highlighted area took on the appearance of the rest
of the strand. Her uncle opened his eyes and looked around. The
medical team stopped the resuscitation and left the room, and
the scene faded. Shiloh rested against the old man, exhausted.
She closed her eyes and inhaled the fragrance that surrounded
them—puppies, peppermint, and pipe tobacco.

The blue-eyed man nodded at Gloriel. The angel sang
a gentle hymn as Shiloh slumbered. The younger man and the
one who sat on the throne listened to her song.

21

Shiloh opened her eyes to the glory of gold ceilings and angels overhead. She sat up and found the blue-eyed man and Gloriel standing near the door where she had entered. The old man stepped down from his seat and joined them. "I have something I need to take care of," he said to the group. He looked at the blue-eyed man. "Would you assist Shiloh on the next part of her journey?" He turned and began walking, disappearing into a softly lit corridor.

The blue-eyed man escorted Shiloh through the door and then into a hallway. They walked in silence to the end of the corridor until they stood before a curtain of amber light. "The next place we'll visit is in a different realm." He took Shiloh's hand and led her through the beam of light. Once they had passed through it, they continued walking until they came to a door made of rectangular sheets of a translucent material. Rays of colored light radiated through them. Shiloh examined the sculpted surface of one of the panels. With her index finger, she traced the outline of a large scale of justice. "What you're about to see is important," he warned. "Are you ready?"

"I am."

He took her hand. The door opened and they stepped quietly into a room paved in alabaster and bathed in candlelight. Gold menorahs hung from the walls. A man who appeared to be a judge sat on a raised bench at the front of the room. Standing at a podium, was Bogren.

Charity stood behind a second podium, facing the judge. "I come before this court to represent my best friend, Shiloh Martinez. I ask the judge to hear my petition on her behalf and render a merciful verdict. Let the record show, that this evil spirit has tormented Shiloh to the point of death. She's suffered from trauma since she was a child. On the day she killed herself, she had not accepted the offer of eternal life. But on that day, she was not in her right mind. She was under extreme mental duress—a state of insanity. I request that she be given a chance to have her life restored, if that is her wish, and if it is the will of the Father." Charity looked at Bogren with contempt.

The judge looked at the demon. "How do you answer?"

"This woman, Charity McBride, is a nothing but a liar. She is a deceiver, a murderer, a fornicator, a blasphemer against God, and a treacherous woman who deserves death for her wicked ways. She has no right to represent anyone in this court. If Miss Martinez wishes to present her case, let her appear in court on her own behalf. I have done nothing wrong. I am perfectly within my legal rights to pursue whomever I want if they make themselves available to me."

"What is your response?" the judge asked Charity.

"Your Honor, as always, the blood of the lamb covers all my sins." Charity turned toward Shiloh who stood at the back of the courtroom. "Your Honor, I would ask the court to allow Shiloh to answer for herself."

"Permission granted," the judge replied.

Shiloh went forward to meet Charity at the podium. "Wait, Charity… what's this all about?" Shiloh asked. "And how did you get here?"

"There isn't time to explain everything," Charity said. "Here's what you need to know for right now. That demon over there is about to accuse you of all the things you've done wrong. Just listen to his accusations and respond to them. I'll be here to help you. Are you ready?"

"I guess so."

Charity looked at the judge. "We're ready to proceed."

The judge looked at Bogren. "What is your accusation against Miss Martinez?"

"Your Honor," the demon said proudly, "you know as well as I do that Shiloh has served the kingdom of darkness her entire life. She's never cared a whit about heaven. She's never done anything to help anyone but herself. She has no compassion or love for anyone. Like her friend, she's a fornicator, an adulterer, a hate-filled murderer of unborn children… a drug dealer, bent on destroying her own life. And since she's determined to destroy her life, I'm only doing my part to help. That foolish woman deserves no mercy from this court."

Shiloh took in the accusations. "It's all true," she said softly to herself. "I'm a terrible person." She turned to Charity. "What should I do?"

"It's simple. In this court, you have two options. Your first option is to do nothing. But you'll be found guilty and he'll win," she said glancing at the demon.

"I'd rather not be found guilty, but I *am* guilty, right?"

"We're all guilty," Charity replied, "but we can choose to be forgiven. Option two is to accept the death of Jesus as the payment for your sins. *He* takes your guilt. *You* become innocent."

Shiloh looked intently at the blue-eyed man, standing at the back of the courtroom. "Okay… then I choose to accept his death as the payment for my messed up life."

"Good choice," Charity said. "Now, tell the judge."

Shiloh turned toward the judge. "Your Honor, I can't deny the accusations. They're all true. But I choose to let the blood of Jesus be my defense."

The judge banged his gavel. "I find you not guilty. Angels, remove this demon from the courtroom."

Bogren cursed loudly as two angels dragged him through a dark passageway leading from the room. "Thank you, Your Honor," Shiloh replied."

Shiloh walked with Charity to the back of the courtroom. Charity looked at the blue-eyed man. He smiled at her. She turned to Shiloh. "Look, sis… I know you must be wondering about all this. I'll explain later, after you come back. I mean… if you come back." She looked at the blue-eyed man, and then back at Shiloh, "I'd better be going." Charity hugged Shiloh, then turned and walked to the door where they entered. She opened the door and disappeared.

22

The blue-eyed man turned to Shiloh. "I'd like to show you something else when you're ready."

"I think I'm ready," she said, shaking her head slowly, adding, "this is so bizarre." She placed her hand in his and he led her out of the courtroom, then back through the amber light at the end of the corridor. They walked across the coliseum floor, where they came to a different corridor and yet another door. This one was made of heavy timber with coarse grain. A large sunflower had been carved into its face; the hinges were carved with ladybugs.

The blue-eyed man stretched out his arm, and the door opened. Before them was a lush landscape of flowers, grasses, and trees. He led her down a smooth stone path that meandered through a meadow. She tugged on his hand, and they stopped. She bent down to look at a flower that radiated light in hues of purple and red. Drawing closer, she heard the faint sound of music. "A singing flower!"

"All the plants have voices. And they do love to sing."

She touched one of the flower's petals. Joy passed through her body. "Incredible."

He gently tugged her hand. "Come this way. I need to show you something."

She walked silently beside him. After walking a short distance through the meadow, they crested a ridge that overlooked a valley. Another hill could be seen in the distance. A glowing light coming from thousands of beings below illuminated the valley in rays of blue, purple, red and gold.

"This is the Valley of Testimony. All these people that you're seeing will come home, into my kingdom because of the story you're going to share with them if you decide to return."

Concern filled her eyes. "Are you saying that they *won't* come here if I don't return?"

"Not exactly. It's a little bit more complicated. If you decide to return, and if you live out your life as it has been planned, they will come here because of the impact your life will have on them. But if you decide to remain here, some of them may still find their way here through the testimony of others."

He turned, and they continued walking in silence through the meadow, bordered on its downhill side by a massive garden of flowers, herbs, shrubs and trees. They crested another hill where he stopped and looked into her eyes, which showed signs of both wonder and worry. "Shiloh, you need to know how much I love you," he said.

She smiled. And then she recalled some of the other men who said they loved her. Fear gripped her. She broke from his gaze and turned away. Her mind raced. She spotted the garden and began walking downhill toward it. She needed to get away from him. She sprinted toward the garden, slowing as she neared the perimeter and then disappeared into its lush foliage. Making her way through the dense vegetation, she tried to put his words out of her mind. Trees of every kind passed by as she walked. Some were more than five hundred feet tall. Moving through the forest, she saw glimpses of color ahead. Soon, the trees became fewer and flowers dotted the landscape.

"I love you?" she said in disbelief. *Who has ever loved me?* She thought.

As she walked deeper into the garden, only flowers remained. Each was a different size and a different color, and each had their own unique arrangement of petals. The further she walked, the more the garden took on a familiar appearance, as if she had been there before. Or perhaps, she'd heard a story about it when she was a child.

As she walked, she noticed something else. It seemed as if the flowers swayed in her direction as she approached. A large daisy with pale-pink petals and a deep-purple center caught her eye. Shiloh thought she heard a voice. The voice seemed to come from the flower. "You have a familiar fragrance."

She stared in confusion at the giant flower hanging in front of her. "I'm sorry, but… did you just say something?"

The flower next to that one, a deep-red rose, nodded. "Oh, yes. You have a rich fragrance."

"I have a what?" she replied, "a fragrance? Flowers have fragrances, humans have smelly—"

"Yes. Yes, you do." The whole garden interrupted her, all the blooms nodding in unison.

The first one, the pink daisy, swayed lower toward her. "I'm sure other flowers have smelled your fragrance. Perhaps you never noticed."

"This is absurd, but I'll play along. Tell me, what does my fragrance smell like?"

"I would call it a most regal aroma. A fragrance very much like the King himself."

"The King!" she replied, amused. "Wait. Do you mean… the old man?"

"I do. Have you ever smelled him?"

Shiloh recalled sitting beside him on the throne. *Peppermint, puppies, and pipe tobacco.* "He does have an incredible fragrance, doesn't he?" she asked.

The rose leaned closer. "Yes, he does. And you smell just like him. I'm not surprised, though. You *are* his daughter."

"His daughter?" she replied, laughing. "I'm not his daughter. My father was a violent drunk who abused little girls." She paused in thought. *How could the old man possibly be my father?*

"Even if I didn't know it, I could tell you were his daughter just by your fragrance," said the rose.

Shiloh pondered the fact that she was talking to a flower. A flower. A flower who thought she was the daughter of the sweetest old man she'd ever met.

A familiar voice sounded in the distance, calling her name. "Shiloh, where are you?"

Shiloh looked around, "Is there any place where I can hide?"

"Hide?" A tiny bluebell bobbed in her direction. "Why would you want to hide from the King?"

"Because he doesn't know I'm here, and he might be angry."

The voice was closer now, "Shiloh, where are you?"

"Don't be silly. He could never be angry with you."

"You obviously don't know how mean fathers can be."

"*You* obviously don't know the King. Other fathers may be cruel, but not this one. He is gentle and loving."

"Well I'm not convinced that I *am* his child. And even if I were, he wouldn't like me when he found out about my… past."

She said the word with the sudden realization that her past had lost its power. Glimpses of her life review flashed before her eyes. "He already knows about my past, doesn't he?"

"Yes, he does. And he still loves you."

She stood motionless. "You're right. If he knows about the terrible things I've done, I think he really *must* love me, though I can't imagine why." A smile appeared on her face. "I'm over here!" she called. The garden waved as she turned in the direction of the old man's voice.

He made his way through a dense thicket of yellow and white flowers. "There you are," he said laughing. "I see you've met some of the flowers."

"Yes, I have," she said. "They're wonderful. This is a beautiful garden you've got, here."

"Thank you, Shiloh. I'm glad you like it, but it isn't mine. I'm only tending it while the owner is away. I created it years ago. It was a gift to my children. They tended it and made it their home. One day, they left, and they haven't returned. So I'm taking care of it until they do."

"Why would anyone ever want to leave this place?"

"Well," he said, "they thought I was angry with them. And they decided that they couldn't live here anymore wondering if I might punish them. Can you imagine that?"

"I think I can," she said. "I felt the same way a few minutes ago."

"You were afraid? Of me?"

"Yes. I was afraid, and I didn't want you to find me. Because I thought you were angry. Because… that's how fathers are."

"Do you think I'm your father?"

"I'm not sure… maybe. I could see you being my dad. You're the kind of dad every little girl needs. But I don't know if that's something *you* want. Because I'm not exactly a perfect daddy's girl. I'm kind of a mess, actually. And what dad would want a failure like me for his little girl?"

"It took a lot of courage for you to tell me that, Shiloh. I know there are a lot of fathers who aren't able to give their children the encouragement and love they need. The world is full of broken people. And broken people don't always do the things they should. I understand why you might be scared to let another man into your life who asks you to call him 'Dad.' But that is exactly who I am. Long before your earthly dad held you in his arms, I held you in mine. Long after your days on the big, blue planet are over, you're going to be right back here with me. I am your father, Shiloh, and I need you to remember that."

She dropped her head, overwhelmed at the revelation of his love toward her. When she looked up, he held out his arms. She hesitated, and then ran to him. "I love you. *Dad*."

"I love you too, Shiloh."

She gave him a squeeze and then stepped back from him. "I need to ask you a question," she said looking into his eyes.

"Ask away."

"The blue-eyed man. Is he your son?"

"He is. But he's not like the other sons I have. He's one of a kind, that one. Do you know what a *forerunner* is?"

"I think so. It's someone who blazes a trail for others to follow. Like an explorer?"

"Exactly right. He's an example for all my sons and daughters to follow."

"He said he loves me. And when *he* said it… it wasn't like the way *you* said it. *You* said it the way a dad says it. But when *he* said it… it was like he wanted me to marry him. And I thought, how could someone as screwed up as *me* every marry someone as wonderful as *him*? All I would do is disappoint him—the way

I've disappointed everyone else. So when he said he loved me, it scared me, and I ran."

"To the garden?"

"Yes."

"Shiloh, when he said he loved you, how did you feel?"

"At first, I was excited, but then I felt unworthy. I knew I could never measure up to his standards, and I knew it would never work out. I knew I'd fail him, like I've failed everyone."

"I should probably tell you something about that son of mine. He's not like other men. Most people remember all the bad things you've done, but they can't remember any of the good things. They focus on your past—your failures. They can't see what you might do in the future."

"Isn't that the truth?" she said to herself.

"But that son of mine, well, he sees possibilities. He doesn't remember the bad from anyone's past. Not even the mistakes they made yesterday. Go ahead. Ask him what he remembers about your mistakes. He'll tell you he doesn't remember them, and, then, he'll look into your eyes and tell you the incredible things you're going to do next week or next year."

Shiloh laughed. "Okay, then. If that's how he is, we might be a perfect match."

"I think you should give him another chance."

The old man walked with her back through the nodding flowers and the budding trees, through the garden and the meadow, and up the hill to where she had left the blue-eyed man. As they crested the hill, they found him sitting on the ground, chewing on a long stem of grass. He looked up. "You're back."

"I'll leave you two alone," the old man said, as he turned and walked toward the door leading to the coliseum.

"I owe you an apology," Shiloh said.

"For what?"

"For leaving you the way I did. I was rude."

"Are you worried that you hurt my feelings?"

"Something like that."

"Would it make any difference if I told you that you didn't hurt me?"

"Don't you care if someone that you love rejects you?"

"You didn't reject me, Shiloh. I sensed what you felt. I sensed that you felt unworthy. You thought you couldn't measure up to my standards. Couldn't meet my expectations. Isn't that true?"

"Well, yes."

"You rejected yourself, Shiloh, not me. And if you rejected yourself, why would that hurt *my* feelings?"

She pondered what he'd said. "I didn't think about it that way. I did reject myself. Not you, but me." Shiloh thought for a moment, then continued, "Since you seem to know just about everything, you must know that I have a lot of personalities."

"I did notice that."

"Lots of little girls running around inside of me… and a few not so little girls. They're confused about… well… everything. Some of them think you're a demon or the devil. I thought you were just another man I should stay clear of… until I met you. Now I know that you're no devil. It feels like my life has been one big lie."

"In a world filled with lies, the truth can be difficult to find. But when you find it, it can set you free."

"That's what I want most, I think. Freedom."

"You know who I am now, but do the girls know?"

"Some of them, but not all."

He took her hand, and they walked back through the meadow. They stopped before a door, and he looked at her. "Are you ready?"

23

The blue-eyed man stretched out his arm, and the door opened. The old man and Gloriel stood talking, nearby.

"Ready for my next lesson," Shiloh called out. The old man turned from Gloriel and took Shiloh's hand, and they walked through the coliseum. Gradually, the dim light that surrounded them gave way to a blue sky that stretched into eternity. A throne appeared, its feet were rooted in the sparkling gems embedded in the mouth of a river.

The river in front of them bubbled up from beneath the throne. Multi-colored ribbons of water spilled gently over rocks, as the river made its way down the side of a sloping mountain and formed a large, glistening body of water in the distance. Shiloh stood at the edge of the stream and looked at the old man. "Go ahead. It's safe," he said. As Shiloh stepped into the river, joy washed over her. The joy seemed to come from the water itself.

He stepped in and stood beside her. She closed her eyes and reveled in his enveloping love. After a few minutes, she took hold of his hand and began walking downstream. "The river... it almost seems to be alive."

"It is alive, Shiloh. I call it The River of Life."

Shiloh fell silent. She walked beside the old man, following the stream downhill. She took in the love and acceptance emitted from the river, and as she did, her spirit became visibly brighter. Before long, the stream widened to meet the sea.

Shiloh looked at the gleaming body of water before her. "What is this place called?" she asked.

"The Crystal Sea."

He waded until he was waist deep in waves that were more love than water. Shiloh followed him, trying to comprehend the joy, peace, and love that ebbed and flowed all around her. She looked at the floor of the sea and noticed that she was standing not on sand or gravel, but on diamonds, sapphires, rubies and other precious stones. She picked up a handful and examined them.

"They're beautiful!" she said, delighted.

"Would you like to do something really fun? Reach down and pick out a handful of stones. Be sure they're ones you like."

She knelt down and, one by one, picked out a handful of the stones. Holding out a sapphire the size of an olive, she said, "This one is the same color as your eyes. I love it!"

He grinned and waved his hand in front of her. A round doorway appeared out of thin air. "Toss them in," he said. Without hesitating, she threw them in. He waved his hand again, and the portal disappeared. "We should probably be getting back," he said.

She looked at him. "But we just got here. And what about the stones?"

"Shiloh, we've shown you all the things you need to see, at least for now. You have a decision to make." He waded ashore and Shiloh followed. They walked hand in hand up the hill, then followed the path to a door that led back to the coliseum. The old man opened it and led her through. They walked to the middle of the vast, crystal floor where Gloriel and the blue-eyed man waited.

24

The blue-eyed man waved his hand before them. Shiloh watched another scene play out before her. Charity decreed life over her pale body as it lay motionless on a hospital bed.

The blue-eyed man took Shiloh's hand. "It's time to make your decision. You've had a taste of what it would be like if you remain here. You've also seen some of what you must endure if you return. It won't be an easy life, but there is a reward. No one will condemn you or think less of you if you choose to remain here. It's your choice. But there is one last thing you should know before you make your decision. If you choose to return, you're free to come back here and visit us whenever you want."

She gripped his hand and looked into eyes that danced with fire. She said nothing, savoring her last moment with him in silence. Gloriel looked on.

"What would you like to do?"

"I want to go back," she said. "There's too much of my life that is unfinished. You and Dad and all the others aren't going anywhere are you? You're always going to be here, right? And you said I can visit whenever I want. So I think... no, I'm sure. I want to return."

"As you wish," he said, smiling. Shiloh looked again at the scene before them. She heard Charity pleading for her to return.

She whispered softly, "Hold on sis, I'm coming."

A small circle of swirling light appeared beside her. As it rotated, it grew larger, forming the entrance to a tunnel that spiraled below them, out of sight. The blue-eyed man looked at Shiloh. "Just remember, I will never leave you. Wherever you go, I am with you."

"I'll remember." Shiloh turned to Gloriel. "I'm glad you're going with me. I don't think I could do this alone."

"It's an honor to be your companion, Shiloh, but I'm a weak companion, at best. I was overpowered by the demons that attacked you." She looked at the blue-eyed man. "All the armies of hell are no match for him."

"I'll remember that too." When the entrance to the tunnel was large enough for them to enter, Shiloh and Gloriel stepped inside it. Their bodies descended into the swirling light, picking up speed. The now familiar expanse of galaxies whizzed past. The tunnel made a gradual curve to the right.

Shiloh looked into the eyes of her angel. "You know, Gloriel, I feel like this place really is my home."

"Heaven is your home. It's where you were created, and it's what you were created for. Earth is a place you're visiting. You're like a foreigner there. Or maybe, an alien," she said smiling. "We're almost there. Are you ready?"

She looked at Gloriel one last time and gave her a long hug. "Okay. Ready."

Their forward motion slowed, and Shiloh saw the hospital

building coming into view. Descending into it, she saw the emergency department and then the morgue, and finally the cooler where her body lay. Coming back into herself, she felt compressed by the weight of her own flesh. She took a shallow breath, and then another, her body gripped by the icy cold.

25

Shiloh opened her eyes in the pitch dark. Her teeth chattered. Her body lay heavy in the plastic bag. Her arms were stiff, resisting her efforts to move them.

She tried to sit up, but banged her head against the inside of the shelf. The bag clung to her face, stifling her breathing. *Stay calm*, she reminded herself. "Jesus, help." Her voice was barely more than a whisper. "Let me out! Can anyone hear me?" She tried to roll back and forth inside the plastic bag.

A woman in black scrubs bent over a mop outside the morgue. She raised her head and glanced down the hall, first left, and then right. Nothing. She went back to her work, pushing the mop back and forth over the white linoleum.

Shiloh rolled her body against the side of the cooler. The sound echoed in the cool, gray light. She called out, "Please let me out! Don't leave me in here. I'm freezing!"

The woman in the hall stared at the doorway to the morgue. She drew near and looked through the small pane of glass, then turned away quickly and started back toward her yellow maintenance cart.

Shiloh rolled and scratched at the inside of the bag. If she could get on her feet, she might be able to climb out of the cooler. *Breathe, Shiloh. Breathe!* She took a shaky breath in the suffocating shadows. "Help, please, somebody!"

The woman in the hall forced herself to walk toward the morgue. She unlocked the door, came into the room, and timidly approached the cooler. She grabbed the handle of the cooler door and carefully swung it open as Shiloh gained enough momentum to roll off the shelf onto the floor.

The woman shrieked and jumped back. Shiloh cried out in pain, beating against the plastic around her. "Hello? Is someone there? Please, help me! Get me out of here!"

The woman stepped back and froze in place for a moment staring at the moving bag. Hesitantly, she leaned forward and grabbed the zipper near the end of the body bag and yanked it down, revealing a very alive woman, shivering in the dim light.

Shiloh tore the bag down from around her face and panted in the open air. The two women stared at each other, Shiloh shivering, the woman's mouth hanging open. "Thank you," Shiloh gasped, "Thank you so much."

"Oh, honey," the woman said. She reached out and pulled Shiloh to her feet. "Let's get you out of here. My name is Maria, okay? I'm going to try to help you. Can you stand?"

Shiloh leaned against her, clutching the bag around her. "Hi, Maria. My name is Shiloh."

Maria steadied her. "Good, that's good. Are you okay if I step away for a minute?"

Shiloh nodded weakly, with her eyes closed. Maria stepped out of the room and returned with a stack of towels. "Here, out of the bag. You can wrap up in these." Shiloh let the bag drop and pulled a towel under her arms and around her body. Maria wrapped another towel around her shoulders like a blanket. Shiloh's feet stung. "Wait, I'll be right back." Shiloh held on to the wall. Maria hurried down the hallway to a cart filled with clean hospital gowns and linen. She pulled out a pair of black scrubs and brought them back to Shiloh. "Put these on. I'll be in the hall."

Shiloh watched Maria as she walked through doorway of the morgue. *The morgue*, she thought, as she dropped the towels and pulled the scrubs slowly over her head and up around her waist. She rubbed her left forearm and walked to the door, then took one last look around the room. "Thank you," she whispered into the air, and then stepped into the hallway where Maria waited.

Shiloh let Maria take her arm and they walked down the hallway. "Where are we? Why was I in there?"

"Chandler Regional Hospital. I'm not sure what you were doing in there. The front desk should know? It's upstairs. I wish I had a wheelchair for you. Can you walk okay? The elevator is this way."

"I'm okay." Shiloh took jerky steps at first, but her gait improved as they walked down the hall and around a corner to the elevator. Maria pushed the button. When the door opened, they stepped in together. Shiloh stretched and rocked back and forth on the balls of her feet as the car ascended. She flexed her arms.

A moment later, the door opened. Maria gestured toward the desk. "Let's see if they can help you."

Maria and Shiloh approached the desk. "How can I help you, miss?" said woman behind the desk.

Shiloh looked at her, and then around the room.

"Do you need me to stay with you, Shiloh?" Maria asked.

Shiloh seemed dazed. "I don't know where to start."

Maria leaned toward the woman. "I found her. In the morgue. She is alive."

The woman wrinkled her forehead and squinted her eyes. "Excuse me?"

Shiloh laughed. "Right, Maria. I'm alive. Thank you for all your help."

"You're a miracle, you know that? God bless you, honey."

Maria walked away, back to the elevator and her workday. Shiloh looked at the woman behind the desk.

"I need to know how I got here," Shiloh said, still shivering, "and I need help getting home."

The woman behind the desk looked confused. "Can you tell me… why you were in the morgue?"

"I'm so sorry, no. I think I might be a patient. Or at least I was one. My name is Shiloh Martinez."

"If you were a patient, I can look you up." She entered Shiloh's name in the computer. "Miss Martinez, it seems you were a patient, and you arrived earlier today."

"Does it say how I got here?"

"You came in by ambulance to the emergency department."

"How do I get to the emergency department?"

The woman stood up and pointed down a hallway to her left. "Take this hallway to the end, then turn left. You'll find it at the end of that hallway."

"Thank you." Shiloh walked to the end of the hallway and opened the door and went into a large waiting room lined with chairs. A registration desk was straight in front of her. She approached the desk and got the attendant's attention. "Excuse me."

"What can I do for you?"

"I think I was a patient here. I'm a little lost. Can you look up my record and see if I was discharged?"

"Sure. What's your name?"

"Shiloh Martinez."

"Hi, Shiloh, my name is Alice. And yes, I do see that name in the computer, but… I don't think you're the Shiloh that we treated here. The Shiloh we treated by that name is deceased, so it can't possibly be you."

Shiloh felt a trickle of something warm and wet running down her chest. She felt for the spot on her neck with her right hand. Her index finger had fresh blood on it. "Alice, I know how this is going to sound, but I'm the Shiloh Martinez who was pronounced dead earlier today. I just came from the morgue. I came back to life, and Maria in housekeeping got me these scrubs to wear. And I'm bleeding. I need help."

Alice looked confused, but there was no doubt about the blood. "I'll have you see the triage nurse. Follow me." She pushed a button that sounded a buzzer, then got up from her desk and hurried through the door to the treatment area with Shiloh following on her heels. She led her to a triage room. "Go in here, and have a seat on the bed. I'll get the nurse for you." Alice went to the nurse's station. "Sal, we have a problem. There's a lady in the triage room who she says she was treated here earlier today and was pronounced dead. She said her body was taken to the morgue… but she came back to life."

Sal laughed. "That's a good one, Alice. A dead lady who came back to life."

"Salvador, I'm not joking! She has the same name as the patient who died, and she's bleeding. I need you to check on her and find out what's going on."

Sal's expression changed. "Okay, okay, I'll have a look. That's why they pay me the big bucks." Sal walked to the triage room and knocked on the door.

"Come in," Shiloh said.

He opened the door. "Hi, my name is—oh, my God, it's you! How in the hell—lady, you're supposed to be dead!"

"I was. But now I'm alive. I was hoping you could help me." She looked down at her right hand streaked with blood.

"Hang on, I'll be right back." Sal sprinted to the nurse's station. "Doctor Rubens, you remember the stabbing that we coded this afternoon that died? Well, she's back, and she's in the triage room."

"Have you lost your mind?" Doctor Rubens replied. He took off his glasses. "That patient was as dead as dead can be. I don't find this amusing, Sal. Maybe you could get back to taking care of real patients."

"Doctor Rubens, please! Come to the triage room, now!"

Sal rushed back to the triage room with Rubens right behind him. "Alright, Sal but I'm warning you, I'm not in the mood for childish pranks." The doctor stepped into the room and froze. "Well, I'll be—it's you. What are you doing here? You're dead."

"I guess I *was* dead, but now I'm alive. And I'm bleeding," Shiloh said pointing to her neck.

Rubens came toward her. "Let me have a look." He examined a wound on her neck that was dripping blood. "I see the problem. Sal, would you hand me a few gauze sponges?"

Yeah, no problem." He opened a drawer and handed a small pile of dressings to the doctor, who took two of them and folded them in half, then placed them over the wound and held them there with his left hand.

"You've got a nice little incision on your neck that's oozing.

It should stop in a few minutes. You know, miss, I'm sorry, I didn't get your name."

"Shiloh."

"Yes, Shiloh, well forgive me, but this isn't something I see every day. You're ice cold," Rubens said. "Sal, would you get her a blanket from the warmer?"

"I'll be right back."

"You know, Shiloh... I've heard stories of things like this happening... mostly from overly zealous religious people. I never believed them."

"My best friend is kind of like that. She always has some insane story I'm supposed to believe. But I'm beginning to see her differently."

"How's that?"

"I thought she told me about these crazy things because she needed to convince me that I should see things her way. But I realize now that it's because she has a lot of experiences most people don't have."

"Speaking of crazy experiences, I just got done signing your death certificate. Now I have to rescind it."

"Doctor. How exactly did I get here?"

Rubens rubbed his forehead. "Well, if I remember correctly, you were found unresponsive at your home. The paramedics transported you here. We did all we could to save you, but you went into cardiac arrest soon after you arrived, and eventually, we had to stop the resuscitation. I pronounced you dead—and believe me—I didn't make a mistake. Your heart had been stopped for half an hour. There were no signs of circulation and no signs of life. You were dead. And the fact that you no longer are is very disturbing."

"Disturbing?"

"I guess this makes you a miracle. We never discussed miracles in medical school because medicine is a science. It's about evidence and research. It's about treatments that we can prove are effective, empirically. If we could just wish people back to life, we wouldn't need doctors, now would we?"

Miracles. The word reverberated in her mind. Rubens was the second person to call her a miracle. The drive home from Mocha's and the thoughts in her mind just before she stabbed herself came rushing back to her, like a long forgotten dream that had been remembered. "I don't know if I'm a miracle or not, Doctor. Yesterday, I didn't believe in miracles. I didn't really believe in God. But today, I killed myself, and you pronounced me dead. After I died, I went to Heaven—it's amazing by the way. When I got there, I was given a choice to stay or come back. I chose to come back. And here I am. Maybe I am a miracle. I don't know...I guess you'll have to decide that for yourself."

Rubens didn't respond, choosing to wrestle with his beliefs in silence. Sal returned with a blanket and wrapped it around Shiloh. "Thanks," she said to him.

"No problem," he replied, taking his seat.

Shiloh looked at Sal. "Would it be alright for me to make just one phone call?"

Sal handed his phone to her. "You're not under arrest. You can make as many as you want."

"Thanks." She dialed Charity's number and waited for an answer. "Charity... it's me. Are you coming to pick me up or do I have to walk home?" A shout of joy could be heard through the phone. "Yeah, it's really me... yeah, I missed you, too... yeah, it's pretty crazy... I have a lot to tell you, too." Tears welled up in her eyes. "I love you, too." She ended the call and handed the phone back to Sal.

"How's it look, Doc?" she asked.

Rubens pulled the dressing away from her skin and studied the incision. "The bleeding seems to have stopped. Sal, can you dress this up a little better?" Sal grabbed the supplies he needed and began dressing the wound. Doctor Rubens looked at Shiloh. "Are you short of breath?"

"No."

"Any chest pain?"

"Nope."

"Do you feel lightheaded or dizzy?"

"Not really."

"Any neck pain?"

Shiloh rotated her head in a circle. "No."

"Remarkable. Sal, let's get a chest and neck x-ray before we send her home just to be on the safe side."

"Will do, Doc."

Rubens got up and walked toward the door. "If you need me, I'll be at my desk."

Sal applied a dressing to the wound. When he was finished, he checked to see if there were more holes that needed to be patched. "Let me see your arms." Shiloh held out both arms and allowed him to inspect them. He noticed but didn't mention the numerous scars and needle tracks on her wrists and forearms. "There's a small one from the IV the medics started on this arm and another one there, but they look fine. Okay, I guess we're done. Sit tight for a few minutes while I get the x-ray tech in here. Things have slowed down so it shouldn't take long."

"Okay, thank you. Sal, do you know where my clothes are?"

"We don't have them. Your top was cut off, and the rest of your clothes were tossed out. Sorry about that. We have a closet full of donated clothes that you can pick from. You won't be making the cover of any fashion mags, but it's better than nothing." Sal left the room. A few minutes later a woman in pink scrubs came in and took x-rays and then left. Sal spotted her leaving and poked his head in the door again.

"Hey, dead lady. Follow me."

They walked to the clothing closet in a back hallway of the department. Shiloh rummaged through the shirts and pants. "These will work," she said, clutching a pair of gray sweatpants and a hooded jacket that almost matched.

"Good choice. Let's move you to a different room. I need to keep the triage room open for other patients."

"I hate to be a pain, Sal, but I'm starving, and I seem to have lost my purse. Do you think I could get something to eat?"

"I'll bet you are hungry. And I've been meaning to get your personal belongings from security. Tell you what I'll do. Here's the room I'm going to move you into until your friend comes to pick you up. Go in there and change. When you're done, head down to the cafeteria and get something to eat, on me." He pulled a ten-dollar bill from his pocket. "Here, take this," he said, shoving the bill into her hand.

"Oh, no, I couldn't …"

"Take it. I insist. And keep the change. It's not every day I get to buy dinner for a walking, talking miracle lady."

"Thank you, so much. You have no idea what this means."

"Go to the main entrance, and ask at the desk how to get to the cafeteria. I'll get your things and bring them back here."

Shiloh disappeared into the room and came out a few minutes later dressed in the sweatpants and hoodie. Sal was nowhere to be found. She made her way to the waiting room, then back to the main entrance and asked for directions. She went to the elevator which took her to the cafeteria. She grabbed a tray and went to the salad bar. She made a salad, then went to the grill. "What's the special today?" She asked the man behind the counter.

"Chicken parmesan over linguine."

"Sounds fantastic, I'll have that." The cook plated her meal and handed it to her. She placed it on her tray and then poured a cup of tea. She put the tea on the tray and carefully brought it to the cash register. Good evening," said the cashier, "that will be seven-fifty."

Shiloh handed over the ten-dollar bill. The cashier handed back her change, which she stuffed in the pocket of the jacket. "Thanks, have a good evening." She carried the tray back down the hall to the elevator and made her way to the emergency department. When she had found her way back to her room, she closed the door and set the tray down on a stainless-steel equipment stand beside the bed. She got comfortable in the bed and placed the plate in her lap, then devoured her dinner, stopping occasionally to ponder the events of the day. Her mind wandered back to when she last saw the blue-eyed man. When she could eat no more, she closed her eyes and propped her head on her palms. His fiery eyes came clearly to her mind. Tears trickled down her cheeks, landing on what remained of her salad.

26

Charity did her best to keep the speed of the Jeep under the posted speed limit. "Wooohoooo!" She yelled as she made the turn onto Arizona Avenue. "Dad, you are the best. I love you so much! Thank you, thank you, thank you, for giving me my little sister back!" When she entered downtown Chandler, she set the cruise control at twenty-five miles per hour. She waved at the police car at the intersection of Chandler Boulevard. A few minutes later, she pulled into the hospital parking lot. She parked the Jeep, hopped out, and ran to the emergency department entrance. She yanked the door open and walked to the registration desk. "Excuse me, I'm here to see a friend who is a patient."

"Hi, I'm Alice," the woman replied. "What is the patient's first and last name?"

"Shiloh Martinez."

"Yes, she's here. I'll be right back, miss." Alice pushed the buzzer to unlock the door, then got up and went through it to the treatment area. She returned a few minutes later with Sal.

"Hey, Goldilocks! Long time no see. You here to pick up the grateful dead lady?"

"Well, I ain't Sugar Magnolia," Charity replied with a smile. *And I'm no friend of the Devil* she thought to herself. She looked at Sal's face. "Are you doing the no-shave-November thing? Because that peach fuzz is definitely not working in your favor," she said sarcastically. "Is that a touch of gray?" she asked, pointing to his chin. "I have a razor in the Jeep if you want get rid of it."

"Ouch! Tough crowd," Sal said, feigning a look of hurt. "Alright, that's enough comic relief for one night. If you want to see your miracle lady, follow me." He looked at the woman behind the desk. "Alice, can you buzz us through?" Sal and Charity disappeared through the doorway. "Never thought I'd see you again. Especially under these circumstances."

"Where are you hiding her?" Charity asked.

Sal motioned for her to follow him. He walked toward the nurse's station. "We set up a little circus sideshow in the back hallway. We got a man who swallows swords, we got an alligator lady, and we got us a real, live, dead lady who ain't dead no more." He walked around to the other side of the nurse's station, then turned into another hallway. "People are paying good money to see the dead lady. Want a ticket? I can hook you up."

"Is there a discount for retired medics?"

Sal turned his head and glanced at Charity but kept walking. "You were in the biz?"

"Used to be. Not anymore."

They stopped in front of Room 23. Sal slid the door open slightly and poked his head inside. "Hey there, dead lady, you seeing visitors?"

Shiloh jumped up from the bed and threw the door open. She

saw Charity and pulled her into an embrace and began crying. "Oh, my gosh, sis. I missed you so much! I love you!" Charity hugged Shiloh long and hard and savored the reunion. Part of her delighted in the return of her friend; part of her relished the moment as a general would, a hard-fought victory.

"Well," Charity said, "I think you've been here long enough. You ready to go home?"

"Home …" Shiloh said the word as if she had never used it before. "Seems like an eternity since I was there."

"What? You just got here, and now you want to leave? I'm really hurt, ladies. What is it, the coffee, the food? I was hoping y'all would stay the night at the Hotel Chandler Regional."

"Sorry, Sal," Charity said. "It's not personal. I have a special homecoming planned for our guest of honor."

"I get it, I get it. I'll bow out gracefully. Shiloh, I just need a couple of signatures on these forms before you go. He laid the forms on the steel table and pointed to the signature blocks. "Here and here." Shiloh signed the forms, and he handed her a sheet of paper. "These are your discharge instructions. Alright, you ladies have fun tonight. Shiloh, you take care of yourself."

Charity gave Sal a long hug, then a kiss on the cheek. "Thanks, Sal. You're a great nurse and a wonderful human being. I'll never forget you."

"Thanks, Goldilocks. You're a class act. It's been a real pleasure meeting you." He turned to Shiloh. "Good meeting you too. Life takes on a whole new meaning when you come face to face with a miracle. Thanks for letting me be a part of it." Shiloh hugged Sal. She got her purse, then she and Charity walked toward the nurse's station.

Shiloh noticed Doctor Rubens looking at her. "Thanks for everything, Doctor."

He got up and walked over toward her. "Pleasure meeting you, Shiloh. There's a chance you may have complications. If you develop breathing problems, chest pain, dizziness, if you notice bleeding or anything else suspicious, come back here, immediately."

"I'll do that, Doctor." She and Charity walked toward the door that led to the registration area. They passed through and walked to the parking lot. Charity opened the driver's side door. "Hey, do you mind if I drive?" Shiloh asked.

"Fine with me." They switched places and got in. After fastening their seat belts, Shiloh turned the key. She backed the Jeep out of the parking stall and turned toward the exit. When traffic was clear, she pulled onto the road and gunned the engine. Her raven hair tossed in the wind. "You know, Charity, for the first time in my life, I feel alive," she shot her friend a glance, "don't ever sell this Jeep."

Shiloh had a look on her face Charity had never seen before. Confidence. A thousand questions flooded her mind, but she was content to save them for later.

Nice going, Dad, she thought to herself. *You did something amazing with your daughter.*

The work has only begun, Charity, replied the familiar voice. *You've been her friend and her sister, but now she needs a teacher.*

The full moon had risen above the Superstition Mountains, casting an amber glow onto the broken clouds above it. The women drove toward home, followed by a large company of angels. A handful of demons also pursued, keeping a safe distance behind.

27

Drumar sat at a table in the darkened corner of a crowded tavern. Bogren entered, and after scanning the room, spotted him and moved in his direction, taking a seat opposite his mentor. "I heard the news, Bogren," Drumar said.

"I'm sorry, sir," Bogren replied, his eyes locked onto a bug that crawled across the floor. "I don't know what went wrong."

"Is that so, Bogren?" the senior demon asked. "Do you mean to tell me that you have no idea at all why Shiloh is back on earth?"

"What I mean, sir, is that... I thought I had a plan in place that would secure her for our side. But it seems I may have underestimated the tenacity of her friend."

"Underestimated? That, my friend, is a gross understatement. Did you give any thought to how Miss McBride would influence her eternal decision? Did you investigate her? Did you analyze her for even a minute to see what you were up against?"

"No, I didn't. I was entirely focused on Shiloh."

"So you ended up in a court battle, and you lost the case?"

"That's an accurate assessment, sir."

"Bogren! You're smarter than that. You're not like the thousands of useless demons I've had to train. There's no teaching those fools. You're different. I'm proud of the work you've done, and you're capable of doing so much better. If I didn't see such great potential in you, I wouldn't be so disappointed."

"I understand, sir, and thank you. I want to live up to my potential, and I appreciate your patience with me."

"It is you who will need patience now, my friend. Shiloh is still your assignment. And now she has found the light. That changes everything. There is nothing that will test the patience of a tormentor like the fervor of a new convert. If you're going to win her back, you'll need to develop a new plan."

"Suicide is off the table then?"

"It would seem so." Drumar stared at a woman sitting at the bar who was being tormented by another demon. A smile appeared on his face. "Bogren, until now, Shiloh had been dismissive of the spiritual world. But now that she's had a taste of it, she might become too interested. A preoccupation with the spiritual will only help us *if* her understanding can be twisted and used to our advantage. With Charity in the picture, that's unlikely. A time-tested way to discourage interest in true spirituality is to give the subject a frightening experience that makes them want to have nothing to do with it. She'll scurry back to her dead religion faster than you can say Beelzebub. Perhaps you and your friends can give Shiloh a night she'll want to forget."

"That's an excellent, idea sir. And what about Charity?"

"Because she isn't your garden-variety church mouse, she'll be a hard nut to crack. As I see it, you have a couple of options. The first is to recruit enough help to overpower and defeat her. That won't be easy. She's an experienced veteran who has already claimed too many from our side. Get too close to her, and you'll be the next casualty. The other option is to avoid all contact with her. That's certainly safer. If you go that route, you'll need to remain out of sight and only have contact with Shiloh when Charity can't interfere. The cover of night is the safest time to engage, as Charity must sleep eventually."

"I understand, sir. And I appreciate your wisdom. Is there anything else you need from me?"

"No, that will be all. Good luck, Bogren, and *do* be careful." Drumar continued observing the demon as it tormented the woman at the bar. Bogren got up from the table and moved quickly toward the door, then disappeared into the night.

28

Shiloh pulled the Jeep into the short driveway and pressed the remote button for the garage door. She slowly pulled forward until a tennis ball, suspended from the ceiling by a string, touched the windshield. She put the Jeep in park, turned off the ignition, and they both climbed out. Charity met her and gave her another hug. "I still can't believe it!" They walked into the living room.

"I never thought I'd be here again," Shiloh said, sitting down in a chair. Charity knelt down on the floor next to her.

"Shiloh, can you talk about it? Where did you go? What do you remember?"

"I remember everything that happened after I… after I died." She said, still struggling to comprehend what had happened. "There's so much to tell you. I didn't leave the hospital right away. I stayed there for a while. I talked to you in the emergency department, but you didn't hear me or see me. You were too busy praying for me." Her eyes filled with tears. "Thanks for not giving up on me."

Charity reached for a box of tissues. She pulled a few out and handed them to Shiloh.

Shiloh wiped the tears from her eyes. "Thanks. So, after that, I took a trip through a long tunnel with a light at the end of it."

"For real?"

"Yeah. It was crazy. Just like everyone says. The tunnel goes on and on and then you see this brilliant light at the end. And then I came out in this… place. It's hard to describe. You've seen pictures of the Colosseum in Rome, right? Well, imagine one a hundred times bigger. Beautiful stone floors, smooth and shiny. And the walls… the walls were made of this, I don't know… crystal-like material."

"It is an amazing place, isn't it?"

"Oh, that's right! You were there—I saw you in heaven!"

"Might be best if we keep that as our little secret, okay?"

"Okay, I promise. No one would believe me anyway."

"So, what else did you see?"

"I have a freakin' angel! Her name is Gloriel. She's probably around here somewhere."

Charity laughed. "Oh, my, how my little sister has changed."

Shiloh looked at her friend. "Charity. I owe you an apology. You did everything you could to try to teach me about demons and angels, but I wouldn't listen. You were so right, and I was so wrong."

"It's okay. Don't be so hard on yourself. I didn't always believe, either. I was just like you, not that long ago. It doesn't matter what you once believed. What matters is that today you know the truth."

"Thanks. That's what I love most about you. You're the only one who never criticized me. No matter how messed up I got, you always loved and believed in me."

"You're not messed up anymore, sis," she whispered. "Dad has you right where he wants you." She got up from the floor and walked to the kitchen returning with two glasses of water. "So, what do you think of Dad?"

Shiloh took a long gulp. "He's amazing. Just like you said. Warm, lovable, kind… never met anyone like him."

"He's a sweetheart, isn't he?"

"I never would have believed it if I hadn't met him myself."

"Who else did you meet?"

"The blue-eyed man." She paused for a moment and finally said, "Jesus," as if the name had to be forced out of her mouth, against her will. "It's strange how I always kind of… detested that name. I've always believed he was mean and that he hated me. But I was wrong. And those eyes. No one has eyes like him. I can still see his face if I close my eyes. It's like he's right here in front of me."

"He's here with us right now."

"He is?"

"Yeah. He said that wherever two or three of us are gathered together, he's here in our midst."

"When did he say that?"

"It's in the Bible."

"I suppose I need to become a little more familiar with the Bible, huh?"

"Wouldn't be a bad idea."

"The last thing he said before I came back was that he would never leave me. He said we were one."

Charity smiled. "Whenever I have doubts, I close my eyes and put all the fears and anxiety out of my mind. And after a few minutes, I can hear him whispering to me. Sometimes I can see him in front of me."

A serious look came over Shiloh's face. "I saw a valley full of people who were going find their way to heaven because of me."

"No kidding?"

"For real. But only if I came back. It made me realize how much we affect each other. I guess we're like stones. You throw a stone in a lake and it makes a ripple. And then another. And the ripples keep moving, and you never know what they'll touch or change."

"Living stones," Charity said softly. "Diamonds and rubies and sapphires. Precious stones that Dad is putting together to build a house for himself."

"A house for himself… I like that. Oh! I need to tell you about the gemstones."

"Gemstones, huh? You really *did* get a tour, didn't you?" Charity said with a smile.

"You know about them?"

"Oh, yes. I know about them. They got me kicked out of a church."

"What!" Shiloh yelled. "How could gemstones get you kicked out of a church?"

"Well, let's just say that not everyone believes they're from God. And in certain churches, if you tell people they are, you might be asked not to come back."

"That's crazy! Dad took me to a place he called The Crystal Sea, and there were millions of them, covering the bottom. He asked me to pick some out, so I did. Then he made this round opening appear out of nowhere. He told me to throw the stones into it."

"You tossed gemstones into a portal?"

"Yes!"

"Now that is weird. I wonder what Dad has up his sleeve."

A noise came from the kitchen like a small stone being dropped on the floor. "Did you hear that?" Charity asked.

"Sounded like something hit the floor."

Charity got up and walked toward the kitchen. Shiloh followed. She flipped the light switch on and scanned the floor. She noticed a few drops of blood that she missed when she'd cleaned the kitchen, and the hasp that was still broken on the knife drawer. She didn't say anything about them. Nothing was going to spoil this moment.

Shiloh let out a scream. She got on her hands and knees and picked up the stone that had come to rest under the overhang of the kitchen cabinets. "You're not going to believe this," she said, holding the large, blue sapphire stone in her hand. "This is one of the stones!"

Charity stepped closer to get a better look. Shiloh held it up to the light so she could examine it. "Are you sure?"

"I'm positive. Dad asked me to pick out the ones I liked best. I remember picking up this one. Don't you love the shape and color? But... how did it get here?"

"A portal is like a tunnel in space and time. It has two ends. One end is in heaven, and apparently—crazy as it seems—the other end leads to our kitchen." Another noise sounded, like the first, but different. It was higher in pitch.

Shiloh scanned the floor. "That sound was different."

Charity looked down. "Yes... almost like it hit a..." she checked the coffee cups on the counter. "Coffee cup," she said, pulling a large, green stone from one of the cups. "Wow, she's a beauty, isn't she?"

"That's another one of the stones I picked out!"

"You have exquisite taste," she said holding it up to the light. "Can I keep it?"

"Of course!"

"Thanks! You and Dad must have had quite an adventure."

"You have no idea. I've never felt as safe as when I was sitting with him."

"I know exactly what you mean. Nothing can hurt you when you're there with him."

Shiloh stifled a yawn. "It's getting late," she said, looking at the clock on the microwave, "I should probably get to bed. We have plenty of time to talk tomorrow."

They said goodnight and walked down the hallway to their bedrooms. Twenty minutes later, the lights were out. Gloriel took her usual place near the head of Shiloh's bed. She prayed in a most beautiful language. At two o'clock in the morning, Bogren appeared. "You've had your fun, Gloriel, now it's my turn."

"Leave her alone you, pile of filth!"

Bogren displayed his claws. "Back off, or I'll give you a matching scar on the other side of your face." Another demon entered the room. Its enormous orange eyes fixed on Shiloh in a menacing glare. A third demon entered. It appeared as a pair of ghostly eyes inside a black hood. It leaned over and whispered in her ear, "Shiloh, come out and play!"

Shiloh sat upright in bed. "I don't know who you are, but get out of my house, now!"

29

The traffic light turned yellow. Ken applied the brake, down-shifted the Harley, and came to a stop. He planted his feet and waved to a young woman entering the crosswalk with two children. When traffic had cleared and the light was green, he accelerated, and, still in first gear, slowed the motorcycle again. He braked hard to avoid hitting a car that cut him off turning into the driveway at Mocha's. He parked the bike near the front entrance, dismounted, and went inside.

A tall, thin man in his forties with spiked, pink hair, wearing a Sex Pistols t-shirt and black jeans stepped to the counter. Shiloh greeted him, "Good morning, sir, how can I help you?"

"How many shots does a large latte have?"

"The standard is three, but I can add as many as you want."

"Can I get six?"

"You only live once. Might as well live dangerously. That will be six-thirty. Do you want that hot, or iced, for here, or to go, and would you like a receipt?"

"No receipt. I'll have it hot, and to go."

Shiloh turned and looked at Tom. "Six-shot, hot latte, to go."

"Six-shooter for the Sex Pistols, coming right up."

Shiloh tried to contain a laugh. "Tom will have that for you at the end of the counter in a minute."

Two firemen were next in line. The younger one turned to the older one, "I got this, Captain."

The captain stepped forward. "Hot, medium, triple-shot latte, to go, please." He moved to the far end of the counter.

The younger man stepped forward. "I'll have the same." He handed her his credit card.

She swiped it and handed it back. "Need a receipt?"

"No thanks." He dropped two dollars in the tip jar, then went to the far end of the counter and waited with the Captain.

"Tina, I need two hot, medium, triple-shot lattes, to go."

"I'll have them in a minute!"

A familiar man came through the door and approached the counter. When his eyes met Shiloh's, her face flushed, and her heart raced slightly. He stepped to the counter. "Aloha."

"If it isn't the man of my dreams," Shiloh said, smiling.

"Wait a sec… I tried that line the last time and went down in flames. What gives?"

"That was then. This is now. You want the usual?"

"The *usual*? I've only been here once."

Shiloh searched her memory but couldn't come up with his order from the previous visit. *Dad*, she thought, *can I get a little help?* A thought popped into her mind. *Large mocha.*

"Hey, Tom, the Big Kahuna needs a large mocha." She thought for a second. "Make it for here."

"You remembered," he said, pulling a ten-dollar bill from his wallet, studying her face.

"It's on me," she said, taking his hand in hers to resist his offer to pay—holding onto to his hand longer than was necessary.

Tom placed a cup on the end of the counter. "I got a six-shot latte, to go!" The pink-haired man picked up his cup and made his way to the door.

Ken walked to the corner booth, carrying his helmet. He took a seat, looked at Shiloh, then pulled out his phone and set it on the table. Shiloh walked over to the espresso station. "Tom, can we switch places for a minute?"

"Sure thing." Tom went to the register while Shiloh made Ken's mocha.

When she had prepared his drink, she carried the yellow porcelain cup to the corner booth and set it down. Beside it, she placed a napkin with a phone number on it. Ken looked at Shiloh and then at the coffee cup. A heart with an arrow through it floated in the foam.

30

As Shiloh slept, she dreamed. Her eyelids rested, still, in the darkness.

Shiloh soared over the water. Her speed slowed, until she came to a place where the water was still and she hovered there. Ken's face floated before her instead of her own reflection. Waves from nearby began to distort his features. Still some distance from her, the blue-eyed man's head broke the surface of the water. "It's you," she said. The blue-eyed man swam toward her, then waded ashore.

He got up and walked away from the river. "Shiloh, come with me. I want to show you something." She got up and followed him, but he took her hand and walked beside her. "What do you know about the gates here?"

"I know they must have some purpose… some meaning."

"What does a gate do?"

"It's a place where you can go in or out. Like a point of access."

"Your inner world has many gates. Each one is different. If each is different, what does that tell you?"

"Each has a different purpose?"

He took her hand and walked toward the bent and disfigured frame of a gate. Crystals lay discarded, half-buried in the dirt. "What do you see?"

"Something that was once beautiful. But it's been ruined."

He turned to face her. "Look into my eyes. What do you feel?"

She gazed into his eyes. A spark of excitement leaped inside her. It kindled a fire that spread warmth through her body which became a roaring inferno in her soul. "Love. I feel loved. Loved in a way I've never felt before. Not sexual love. Pure love. Real love. Like I'm accepted, just the way I am."

"Shiloh, I accept you. And I do love you just the way you are."

"I know you do."

A loud motorcycle rumbled by the house, disturbing Shiloh's sleep. She rolled over and a moment later, was back in the dream.

"This," he said pointing to the ruins, "is your love gate. If you're unable to give or receive love, it's because this gate has been damaged." He bent down and picked up a red piece of crystal, then held it up to a heart-shaped hole in the framework of the gate. "Needs a bit of work." He knelt down and scooped a handful of mud and dribbled it over the crystal as he held it in place. He let go and the crystal transformed to fit the heart-shaped opening perfectly.

She picked up a blue piece of crystal in one hand and a handful of mud in the other. "Does it matter where they go?"

"It's your gate."

She held the crystal up to a hole in the framework, dribbled some mud over it and then let go. The crystal fell to the ground.

"Try again."

"I don't think it goes there." She picked up a purple crystal and more mud, then held it in place as she let the mud flow over it.

"Tell me what's going to happen when you let go."

"It's going to fall to the ground."

"Oh, ye of little faith," he said, laughing. He placed his hands on hers. "What's going to happen when we let go?"

"It's going to stay there."

"Are you certain?"

"I believe so."

They lifted their hands, stepped back, and watched as the crystal transformed to perfectly fit the opening. "Nice going! Now we need to do something about the frame."

"Any ideas?"

"You could repair it. Picture in your mind what the gate should look like, then speak it into existence."

"Gate, be made new!" Instantly, she watched the metal bars rise and take the form of a shining gate.

"Well done," he said. "Now, let's put the stones in place."

Shiloh picked up a yellow stone and held it in place, then dripped mud over it. She let go, and it morphed to fit the shape of the hole. She set another stone in place and then another. Before long, mud began flowing slowly toward the gate, being carried by a steady trickle of water. With each piece of crystal set in place, the flow of water increased until it became a cool, clear stream flowing toward the woods beyond the gate.

31

Shiloh stood at the kitchen counter, her hands inside a mixing bowl, kneading dough. She tossed some flour onto a cutting board, then dumped the ball of dough out and shaped it into a flat circle. She pulled out a glass pie pan from the cupboard and set it on the counter, then carefully folded the circle in half, and then again in half. She picked it up and laid it carefully into the pie pan, then opened it up so that it hung over the edges of the pan. She poured in the filling which she had prepared earlier and then took a second circle of dough and laid it over the top. She crimped the edges, then basted the top with egg wash.

Charity walked into the kitchen. "What's for dinner, sis?"

"Chicken and dumplings with peach pie for dessert."

"That sounds delicious."

"I was hoping to have Ken over tonight. He mentioned the other day that he loves Southern food."

"Ken? Coming here?" Charity studied Shiloh.

"If it's okay with you? I still need to call him and make sure."

"Absolutely! I'd love to meet him. You've been dating for a while and I sense you're getting serious. How much have you told him about your past... and the girls?"

Shiloh looked up at Charity, and stared past her, vacantly. Charity braced herself for whoever would come up next, but Shiloh blinked and kept talking. "We had some really long talks and I told him just about everything."

"Would it be okay if I talked with him? I don't want to interfere. You know I want what's best for you. I'd just like to know his thoughts about the girls."

"That's fine. I trust you," Shiloh said. "Speaking of trust... any chance you could unlock the knife drawer for me?"

Charity removed the lock. Shiloh opened the drawer and looked at the knives, then selected one of medium length. She cut holes in the top crust of the pie, then washed and dried the knife and put it back in the drawer. Next, she removed a kettle from the cupboard and set it on the stove. She opened the refrigerator and took out two chicken breasts, carrots, and celery stalks and laid them on the counter. She sprinkled pepper and salt on the chicken, then took another knife from the drawer and began to chop them.

Charity let out a slow breath and smiled. *She's different, Dad. Yes, she is.*

32

Hector, Ken's assistant called to him from the end of a long aisle, "Hey, Ken, how many of these two-by-twelves do you want?"

"Fifteen, can you help load them on the cart?"

Ken went to the service counter to pay for the lumber. Hector helped an employee pick out the straightest boards and load them on the cart, then pushed the cart toward the open door where Ken waited for him. "Let me flag these bad boys, and we're good to go." Ken tore off a red piece of plastic from a roll and stapled it to the end of one of the boards.

In the parking lot, Hector and Ken guided the cart to the flatbed work truck. Ken pressed the remote and unlocked the doors, while Hector lowered the tailgate. The two men loaded the boards into the truck and secured a tie-down over them, then headed toward the cab. Ken's phone rang. "Aloha, baby." Hector grinned and jumped in the cab to wait for Ken.

"Hi, Ken."

"What's up, Shiloh? Nice to hear your voice."

Shiloh cleared her throat. "It's nice to hear yours, too. Hey… I was wondering if you have plans tonight. I'd like to have you over for dinner to meet Charity."

"Sounds great. I need to drop off a load of lumber at the Power Road jobsite and then take the truck back. After that, I'm free. I'd love to meet you and Charity for dinner. What time should I be there?"

"How does six-thirty sound?"

"I'll be there, with bells on."

"See you then."

"Aloha."

Ken ended the call and stuffed the phone in his pocket, then climbed into the cab. He started the engine and pulled the truck out of the parking lot. They headed east on Baseline Road. "Hot date tonight?" Hector asked.

Ken smiled to himself but didn't answer.

"Shiloh?"

"Good guess." The traffic light turned yellow. Ken brought the truck to a stop. "Never met anyone quite like her."

"Sounds serious."

"It's beginning to look that way, amigo." When the light turned green, Ken continued driving east toward Power Road.

33

Ken approached the driveway. As the Harley went through the gears, he flipped the turn signal on, guided the motorcycle into the driveway, lowered the kickstand, and shut off the engine. After dismounting, he opened the compartment over the rear fender, stowed his helmet and gloves, then pulled out his phone and verified the house number. A whiff of freshly baked desert caught his attention. "Peach pie," he said with a smile. He knocked twice, then ran his hands through his black hair, streaked with silver. The time he'd spent on the islands had etched a gentle map of laugh lines into his face. A string of cream-white sea shells hung around his neck. Mocha skin and espresso-bean eyes completed the portrait of a man who worried about nothing. The door opened. "Aloha."

Shiloh gave Ken a long hug and a kiss on the cheek. "So glad you could make it."

"Wouldn't miss it for the world. How you feeling?"

"A little headache, but nothing terrible. I'll get through it.

Come on in." She turned to Charity. "Ken, this is Charity, my roommate, boss, and my very own personal barista."

Ken reached out to shake her hand, but Charity wrapped him in a long hug. "So nice to meet you."

"Aloha, Charity," Ken said as he hugged her. "Thanks for having me over."

Shiloh walked toward the dining room. "Ready to eat? Let's sit down while it's still hot." She pulled a chair out for Ken, then sat beside him.

Charity sat down and looked across the table at Ken. "Shiloh tells me you lived in Hawaii most of your life. How did you end up here, in the middle of the desert?" Charity ladled chicken and dumplings into her bowl while Ken talked.

"It's a long story. But I'll give you the condensed version. I was actually born here, in Arizona. My dad joined the Navy, and when I was three we moved to Oahu. Loved growing up on the island. I learned to surf and sail, but I knew I'd never make any money doing it. I've always liked business and finance. So, when I graduated high school, I went to the University of Hilo. Got my MBA and a BA in finance. My first job out of college was with Merrill Lynch, but I had to leave the island. I made a ton of money in a short period of time, but it's a cutthroat business, and I hated it. So, I left the firm and worked for different financial groups around the country. Those were the most frustrating years of my life. One day, an old buddy from Honolulu called and asked how I was doing. I told him things were okay, financially, but I hated the company I was working for. He'd started up a business and needed help with the financial end of things, and offered me a job. I went into work the next day, told them I was leaving, and caught the next plane to Honolulu. I worked for my buddy for the next seven years. It was a great gig, and I'd still be there today, but half my family is here in Arizona and they asked me last year to help them with their own business startup. I moved back here to help get their business off the ground. It's doing well, but I'm looking forward to turning it back over to them and getting back to what I really want to do."

"And what is it you really want to do?" Charity asked.

"Move back to Hawaii. Settle down with a good woman. And sell overpriced coconuts to wealthy tourists."

"Think you'll make any money?" Charity took a bite of chicken and dumplings.

"Probably not. The coconut market is overleveraged. But my old job in Honolulu is waiting for me when I'm ready to go back."

Charity looked at Shiloh. "You gonna ditch me to live with this guy in Hawaii?"

Shiloh smiled. "If you don't pass me the chicken and dumplings, I might."

Charity passed the serving dish to Shiloh, then she looked at Ken. "I'd like to ask you a couple of questions. And I hope this doesn't make you defensive. I'm only asking because I care about Shiloh and I don't want to see her get hurt… or you. As you know, the multiples can make life a little challenging. The men she's dated haven't been able to deal with her alters. I'd like to hear your thoughts on that."

Ken laid down his spoon, and wiped his mouth with the white cloth napkin. He looked at Shiloh and then back at Charity. "Shiloh isn't the first person I've known who has multiple personalities. My mother is a survivor, so I know the difficulties. It's a challenge, but no one's guaranteed an easy life, are they?"

Charity smiled. "Seems like maybe you've been prepared for this." She looked out the window at the mountains as the last rays of sun bathed them in gold. "I'm not surprised," she added.

34

November winds bring tamer temperatures to the Valley of the Sun. Situated on the south bank of the Salt River is Tempe Marketplace. Rust-red cobblestones form a wide walkway dividing two rows of storefronts. Meticulously groomed palm trees shine with festive holiday lights as sunset approaches. A massive stone fireplace in the middle of the mall beckons weary shoppers to rest on rattan couches.

"Can we sit down for a minute?" Shiloh asked.

"Sure thing." They sat down on a couch in front of the fireplace. "Anything on your mind?"

Shiloh stared at the flickering, blue flame that danced inside the fireplace. "I've been thinking about some of the things I saw in heaven."

"Like what?"

"As soon as I arrived there, I went into this large ball and saw a review of my whole life. I realized that I never tried to help anyone else. When we were in court, that demon accused me of being selfish. He said I had no compassion for anyone—never helped anyone. And he was right."

"After all you've been through, sis—"

"Please don't," Shiloh interrupted. "Don't make excuses. When I first met Jesus in the dry places, I felt something I'd never felt before. I felt… like I had to help others… like the only thing that mattered was taking away their pain. Look, I've been given a second chance at life and I don't want to screw this up. You seem to naturally want to help other people and I was hoping you could show me how I could be more like that. More compassionate."

Charity stared at Shiloh in shock. *Okay, Dad,* she thought, *any suggestions?*

A thought seemed to answer her, *He saw a great multitude, and was moved with compassion for them, and healed those who were sick.*

"I have an idea," Charity said.

"I'm all ears."

"One way I demonstrate compassion is through healing. Jesus healed thousands of people because he had compassion on them."

"But he was Jesus, and I'm not."

"That's true, but he gave us the authority to do the same things he did."

"Like healing?"

"Healing, signs and wonders, removing demons—"

"Sounds exciting," Shiloh said, "and… maybe a little scary."

"It's not as scary as you might think. And I can show you how to avoid the pitfalls."

"How does it work?"

"Creative miracles are done by releasing power. We're like rivers. We carry the power of heaven inside of us. We open the gate and let the power flow out."

Shiloh closed her eyes. In her mind, she watched as a torrent of water flowed beneath a silver gate into the surrounding countryside. "I think I understand," she said.

"We can also use authority and command sickness to leave. How about a little practice?"

"Right now?"

"Why not?" Charity got up from the couch. "Okay, see that boy over there, standing by the fountain with his arm in a sling?"

Shiloh got up. "The one with the blue shirt? Yeah, I see him."

Bogren had been watching from a distance, but drew near. "So you think you're a miracle worker, do you? Don't make me laugh, you silly human! Please *do* go and pray for someone. I'm going to relish your disappointment when nothing happens!"

"What if we practice healing on him?" Charity asked.

"I don't know if this is a good idea," Shiloh said. "What if nothing happens?"

"That's right, my dear," the demon whispered. "You should consider this carefully, because when nothing happens, the whole world will know you're a fraud."

"There's never any guarantee that a person is going to be healed when you pray for them," Charity said.

"But if I pray for him and nothing happens, I'm going to look like an idiot."

"You *are* an idiot if you think you're going to get anyone healed," Bogren replied.

Charity suddenly felt fear and dread. Closing her eyes, she scanned the area until she saw Bogren's dark form. She directed her thoughts at him. *Get lost, now!* The demon quickly retreated toward a row of trees at the edge of the mall.

"Why don't I pray for him, and you watch?" Charity asked.

"Deal," Shiloh said, smiling.

They walked nearer to the fountain and took a seat at a table. No sooner had they sat down than the boy came over and sat next to them. He began talking with his mother. When there was a break in the conversation, Charity got the woman's attention. "Excuse me, ma'am. I'm teaching my friend here about healing, and I was wondering if you'd allow us to pray for your son to be healed."

She looked at her son, then back at Charity and Shiloh. "Are you healers?"

"We are."

"What kind of healing do you use?"

"It's all Jesus, ma'am."

"Oh, that would be wonderful. Derrick, would it be alright if these women prayed for your arm to be healed?" The boy smiled and nodded his head. "He's a little shy, but once he warms up to you, there's no quieting him down."

"Hi, Derrick," Charity said. "Does your arm hurt right now?"

"Yes," he replied, "mostly when I lift it up."

"Can I ask what happened to your arm?"

"I fell off the monkey bars at school."

"Is it okay if I pray for you?"

"Sure, I guess."

Charity placed her hand a few inches from the boy's elbow. "I command this arm to be completely healed. I command bones, ligaments, tendons and nerves to be healed. How does your arm feel, now?"

He tried to raise his arm. "It still hurts."

"Let me try again, " Charity said as she placed her hand near the boy's arm.

As Shiloh watched, a spark of compassion ignited inside her and spread like a wildfire.

"I command bones, nerves, tendons, ligaments and cartilage to be healed," Charity said. "How does your arm feel now?" The boy tried to raise his arm, "It still hurts."

Shiloh spoke up, "Can I try?"

"Why not?" Charity replied with a grin.

Shiloh placed her hand near the boy's arm, closed her eyes for a moment, then whispered in Charity's ear. "There's a dark spirit near his elbow."

Charity whispered back, "In your mind, tell it to leave."

Shiloh directed her thoughts at the spirit, *Be gone, now!* The spirit vanished. Shiloh looked at Derrick. "How does your arm feel now?"

He raised his arm above his head. A look of surprise appeared on his face. "Hey! It doesn't hurt!"

"Thank you… thank you both for your time," the boy's mother said. "God bless you."

Charity got up from her chair and shook hands with the boy and his mother, "It was very nice meeting you. Thank you for letting us practice."

Shiloh and Charity walked back toward the fireplace, then sat down on a couch. Shiloh stared into the flickering flames, "I can't believe it. He actually got healed."

"And we made a demon homeless," Charity added.

35

Drumar stood beside the hospital bed observing the nurses and doctors. A man in his fifties lay in the bed. One by one, the hospital staff left the room until only one nurse was left. "Get out," Drumar whispered in her direction. The nurse looked at the monitor, then jotted down the numbers and left the room. Drumar placed his hands around the man's throat and squeezed tightly. The man began breathing more deeply. Drumar tightened his grip. Perspiration appeared on the man's face. His breathing became faster and more labored. The demon held his grip. The man's lips turned dusky-blue, and his breathing slowed. Drumar smiled. "That's right. Don't fight it. It'll be over soon."

A red light illuminated on the monitor, while an alarm rang at the nurse's station. A voice crackled over the intercom, "Code blue, room eight! Code blue, room eight!" The staff who had just left, returned. A tall, muscular man slid a plastic board under the man's chest, checked for a pulse, then began CPR. The team began resuscitating the patient. Bogren watched. Drumar gave him a knowing smile and then released his grip on the man's throat. "I think my work here is done." Drumar and Bogren took their conversation into the hallway.

"I've never seen you in the trenches, sir. If I may say so, you do excellent work."

"Thank you, Bogren. As a rule, I don't like getting my hands dirty. I've put in my time. But this was a special situation. As you know, our tormentors have been unusually busy. The agent assigned to this one was needed elsewhere. I considered sending a replacement, but I have a personal history with this chap. It made for an opportunity to even the score. And I do hate to see a good opportunity wasted. Turns out I got here just in time. Barring a miracle, I believe Mister Paul Martinez will be joining us down below momentarily."

"Did you say Martinez?"

"I did. And, yes, Mister Martinez is Shiloh's uncle."

"Thank you, sir. I feel like you've done me a personal favor."

"And now you can repay the favor." Drumar walked in the direction of the waiting room. "I received your latest report on Shiloh," he said. "You must realize now, she's no longer a passive participant but an engaged enemy. This changes everything. You'll need to employ different strategies and tactics."

"Yes, of course."

"Well, what have you come up with?"

"She's become aware of her authority, and she's exercising it. She managed to banish a spirit of pain. Obviously, that puts me in danger. I'll have to be more careful about how I interact with her. And of course, I'll need to avoid being detected by Charity."

"Go on."

"Shiloh has more confidence. That's a problem. I could attack her confidence—make her feel weak and useless. Or I could tempt her into becoming over-confident—get her hopes up and when things don't go as expected, she'll be devastated."

"Both options are worthy of consideration. But you *do* realize that defeating her confidence won't be easy with Charity at her side. Her encouragement is an annoyance I can't bear to watch. Getting Shiloh to overestimate her abilities with a little spiritual judo may be the better plan. You might give both options a try and see which one holds more promise. Let me know how things go."

"I'll do that, sir." Bogren turned, went down the hallway and disappeared through the hospital wall.

36

Shiloh sat in a chair staring out the window. "I had a strange dream last night."

Charity was curled up on the couch reading her email. "Care to tell me about it?"

"I was in an art gallery that was filled with beautiful paintings. I went from one painting to another, looking at how each one captured a certain light or shadow or a mood. Each time I looked at a different painting, I felt like I'd seen it before. I couldn't remember when or where but every painting had a familiar look to it."

"Anything else happen?"

"In another scene, I was in something like a classroom. There was a man at the front of the room. He was standing there smiling at me, then he asked me to come to the front. So I got up and walked over to him. He opened a glass jar that had swirling colors inside. I couldn't tell what the colors were made of, but he reached in with his hand and scooped out some of the colored stuff and placed it on my head. Then it ran down over me and dissolved into me."

"Interesting dream. How did you feel when the colors were running down over you?"

"I felt… like they were becoming a part of me."

"How did you feel when you were in the gallery?"

"I felt a sense of awe. The paintings were exquisite. They seemed to be carefully planned out, if you know what I mean. Each composition was different, but there was a sense of unity. They fit together like a collection."

"I've never heard you talk that way about art. Where did *that* come from?"

"I've always been interested in art. I've even tried taking some classes and workshops, but I never finished them because I always ended up in treatment."

"Maybe Dad is telling you something in the dream."

"Like what?"

"Why you're here and what you're supposed to be doing."

"You think Dad wants me to be an artist?"

"It might sound crazy, but humor me. How would you feel if those were *your* paintings?"

"Well, I guess… I would feel like I'd finally found what I'm supposed to do with my life."

"Could you imagine being an artist?"

"I don't see how that could ever happen."

"I know. But just try to imagine it for a minute."

Shiloh's eyes welled with tears. "If those were my paintings… I think I'd be the happiest person on earth."

"I never knew you were so interested in art. Friends aren't supposed to keep secrets like that."

"I think most of what God put inside me is buried under piles of sorrow. I love art. But I never had a chance to take it seriously. I spent so much time running from people who wanted to hurt me." She got up from her chair. "If I *did* want to be an artist, where would I start?"

"What if you pick up where you left off?," Charity said. "If you need details, you should talk with Dad." Charity turned and walked to the large window that faced toward the mountains and stood there in silence.

A familiar voice spoke, *What about Janet?*

What about Janet? Charity thought.

She's a painter, and she loves to teach.

Charity turned toward Shiloh. "I have a friend who lives in Tempe. She's a painter. I wonder if she'd consider doing a little mentoring."

"I don't know if that's a good idea. I don't know her, and she doesn't know me."

"Shiloh… if you have a little faith in Dad's ability to connect you with the right people, you might be surprised at how well things work out."

"How have things worked out for me so far?"

"Well. You were dead a few days ago, and now you're alive. If he can pull *that* off, I think he can work this out."

Shiloh smiled. "Hard to argue with that. It would be a dream come true… literally," she said. "Alright. If you can arrange it, I'd like to meet this artist."

37

Charity drove the Jeep westward on Highway 202 toward Tempe. "You'll like Janet. She's a sweetheart. She's laid-back, and she's a believer, so if you have any questions about Dad you can ask her."

"I can't believe I'm doing this!" Shiloh yelled, so she could be heard over the road noise.

Charity exited the freeway. A few more turns, and she parked the Jeep in front of a pale-yellow, stucco house. They got out and went to the front door. Charity rang the doorbell. A petite, middle-aged woman with brown hair and blonde highlights wearing a gold sweater, cream-colored leggings and leather boots answered the door. "Hi, Charity!" the woman said as she gave her a hug.

"Hello, Janet. This is my friend, Shiloh. She's the one I told you about."

"Hi, Shiloh," she said, shaking her hand, "come on in, and make yourselves comfortable."

Janet's house was modern and tastefully decorated with original paintings on the walls. Shiloh stopped in front of one painting that was an abstract in earth tones with a jagged, vertical streak of gold running through it. "This is beautiful. Did you paint it?"

"Yes, I did that one many years ago. My work has changed a lot since then. I'm focusing more on landscape painting, now. Our mountains, and the sky, are an endless inspiration."

"If it's all right," Charity said, "I think I'll leave you alone to get better acquainted. Shiloh, how about if I pick you up in a few hours?"

"That's fine. I'll text you when I'm ready to come home. Is that okay with you, Janet?"

"Sounds great."

Charity went to the front door and let herself out, while Janet and Shiloh continued talking.

They walked to the back of the house and down a hallway toward a door that opened to her studio. Against one wall of the large, bright room were racks that held canvases. Two large easels stood in the middle of the room, surrounded by tables covered with painting supplies and brushes. Janet pulled out a stool for Shiloh. "Charity has told me a little bit about your history… and she's noticed your love for doodling."

Shiloh smiled. "It relieves the boredom when things are slow at work… and I think it helps me process life."

"When life gets out of control, art can be a retreat for the soul. Today, I'd like to get an idea of your skill level. Would you be comfortable doing a simple drawing for me, so we can decide where to start?"

"I'd like that."

Janet pulled a pad of newsprint paper and a charcoal pencil from a shelf and handed them to Shiloh. She placed a ceramic coffee mug on the table in front of her. "Let's start with this mug."

Shiloh took a breath. She began lightly sketching in the proportions of the mug. She added the dark areas, and slowly, the mug's form took shape. She continued drawing more detail and added the shadow cast on the table. In ten minutes, she had the drawing complete. Janet looked at it. "Very nice."

"Does this mean I have potential?"

"Yes. You're off to an excellent start. I can certainly teach you a few things, but you already have a good sense of light, shadow and proportion."

Shiloh looked at the rack of paintings against the wall. "Would you show me some of your paintings?"

Janet got up and walked to the vertical racks. Shiloh followed. Janet carefully pulled out several paintings and leaned them against the wall.

"These are beautiful. I would give anything to be able to paint like this."

Bogren slipped silently through the wall. "Who are you kidding, Shiloh? You're not an artist. You're a nut job. You belong in a mental institution."

"Let me do a little demonstration for you and then you can give it a try, if you'd like," Janet said.

"Great! I'd love that."

Bogren drew closer. "Shiloh, you're going to fail again like you always do. Your best talent is making a mess of your life."

"I take photos of the mountains for reference," Janet said, "I won't be copying the photograph, I prefer to use it for inspiration. Let me show you how I begin with an underpainting."

"What's an underpainting?"

"It sounds complicated, but it's simple. I use a dark-brown or gray and do a quick painting, blocking in areas with my brush to establish the composition. After it's dry, I'll start adding color, from darkest to lightest. The final highlights are the most fun—the magical finishing touches."

Janet secured her canvas to an easel and squeezed some burnt-umber paint onto her palette. She put the palette down and taped her landscape reference photo to the easel.

"Notice that I'm standing back from the canvas so I can use my whole arm while painting. Think of the brush as an extension of your arm. It also helps to squint. Blur your eyes while looking at the photo. Try it. Can you see the separate areas of dark and light?"

"I can."

Janet picked up the brush and painted the shapes of the mountain shadows first, leaving blank areas where a palo verde tree would eventually emerge in the foreground. "I'm starting with the areas of dark—drawing them with the brush." Janet squinted at the image and continued painting. Then, when she had the darkest areas defined, she thinned her paint, and filled in the medium tones, including the canopy of leaves against the sky. Shiloh watched as the painting took shape.

Janet turned to Shiloh. "Would you like to try?"

"I'd love to."

Janet removed the canvas from the easel and replaced it with another one. "Try holding the brush like this," she said. "When we're doing an underpainting, we don't need to fuss over detail. There's plenty of time for that later. Just use your brush to capture the dark shapes and shadows, first. Relax, and keep your edges soft for now."

Bogren whispered in Shiloh's ear, "There are millions of starving artists in the world who have more talent than you. What makes you think you're going to make any money as a painter?"

Shiloh thought about what the demon had said while she continued painting. "May I ask you a personal question?"

"That depends on what it is," Janet said smiling.

"Would you consider painting to be your career? I mean, do you earn enough from your art to pay your bills?"

"Yes, I've been making my living as an artist for more than twenty years. I'm not rich—but I live very comfortably."

"Maybe the reason I never considered art as a career is that I'd always heard about starving artists. I never thought anyone could make a living at it."

"I used to believe the same thing—especially when I was younger and just getting started. But one day, God challenged me to try selling my paintings. I was surprised at how quickly the first one sold. It wasn't long before I had sold most of my originals. The starving artist myth is just that… a myth… a lie from the pit of hell. There are even self-taught artists who do well selling their work. It seems there's an audience for nearly every kind of art. It's as much about marketing as it is talent."

"Do you think… it would be possible for someone like *me* to be a successful artist?"

"It's plain to see you have a lot of raw talent. That will only improve, the more you paint. I can teach you what I've learned about marketing and working with collectors and galleries. Self-confidence is the main thing you're lacking, but that will grow as you see your skills grow. It takes work, but, yes—if you're determined, of *course* you can be successful!"

Shiloh put down her brush and gave Janet a hug. "You have no idea what this means," she said, her eyes filling with tears.

38

Drumar gazed at the statue before him. Its pale, smooth form, tight musculature, and glinting highlights stood in contrast to the rough texture of Bogren's deformed body which seemed to absorb particles of light that came near it. "So she thinks she's an artist, does she?"

"It would seem so," Bogren replied.

"How did she learn about her destiny?"

"Our enemy gave her a dream."

"Is that so?"

"It's worse, sir. Charity is encouraging her to pursue a career as an artist."

"Does that surprise you, Bogren?"

"Does it surprise me? No… no, it doesn't. Charity is always interfering in my plans. It would be so much easier if she weren't around."

"Bogren, don't turn this into a pity party. This isn't about you. It's about Shiloh. And Charity isn't leaving anytime soon, so you'll have to work a little harder. Our enemy has made their move. Now it's time for us to make ours. We have weapons that are just as powerful as theirs. Perhaps even more so. Shiloh is receiving encouragement from her little friend. What's your best strategy to overcome it?"

"Discouragement?"

"Precisely! In the same way that you overcome peace with fear, you overcome encouragement with discouragement. Discourage her in every way possible. Let her know how hard it will be competing against artists with more talent. Remind her that no one will take her seriously. Remind her of her failures and the times she's been rejected. Let her know more failure and rejection are coming. Remind her of all the hopeful artists who have died depressed, disillusioned, and penniless. She may have hope now, but if you play your cards right, in a few days, she'll be back in treatment, where she belongs. We overcome good only through evil, Bogren. Don't ever forget that."

"Thank you, sir. You've been a great help." The demon turned and left.

39

Shiloh sat on the couch, staring out the window at the sun-washed mountains. "I'm scared."

"I know," Charity replied, "but I won't do anything to hurt the girls, and I won't do anything without their permission."

"What's going to happen to them?"

"That depends on what they want. And what Jesus wants."

"What do you think he wants?"

"I think he wants you to be normal."

"Normal? What's normal?"

"Not being triggered, not being terrorized, and not trying to kill yourself."

"I want that too. I'm better, but I can still feel the girls struggling for control when things get too intense," Shiloh said. "I'm scared, Charity. I don't know who I'll be without them."

"I know you're scared. Change is frightening. But if you never allow change to happen, you and the girls are going to live with the pain the rest of your life."

"But they're a part of me."

"You're right. They are a part of you. But they're a wounded part of you, and they need healing. And once they're healed, they can be a healthy part of you instead of a wounded part of you."

"What will happen to them?"

"That depends. Some will become a part of your core. Others might not be ready for that. They'll remain independent.

"They're not going to be… *annihilated*, are they?"

"No. I promise nothing bad will happen to them."

"Each one gets to decide?"

"Yes. Jesus always asks permission before he does anything."

"I'm scared."

"I know," she replied. "But you know I love you, and you know I would never let anyone hurt you."

"I know," she said. After a long pause, she finally said, "Okay. Let's get started, before I chicken out."

"Okay, here we go." Charity looked in her eyes. "Becky? Becky, if you can hear me, I need you to come up."

Shiloh's eyes fluttered gently for a few seconds, then opened wide. "Well, hey, Charity, how's my girlfriend doing?"

"Hey, Becky, we need to have a serious chat."

"You have my full attention, sugar, and I got all the time in the world."

"Becky, do you know Jesus?"

"You mean… like my personal Lord and Savior?" she said laughing.

"That's the one."

"Well, I like Jesus, because he hung out with the hookers and all, but I'm not too sure he likes me."

"Becky, why don't you ask him? He's standing in front of you."

Becky's eyes studied the blue-eyed man who stood in front

of her. "Well, well, well. What have we here? Are you a friend of sinners, Son of Man, or only a friend to saints?"

"Becky, may I show you something?"

"What do you have in mind?"

He waved his hand and a scene appeared before them—one she had seen before. Shiloh was a little girl, lying facedown on her bed as her father beat her with his belt. What she had *not* seen before was Jesus sitting beside her on the bed, wiping away each tear as it fell. "I've always been here, Becky. From the day Shiloh was born, I've never left her side and I never will. I love her, and I love you."

"If you love us, why didn't you stop him?"

"Do you remember your first boyfriend, Maurice?"

"How could I ever forget that backstabbing son of a—"

"He hasn't forgotten you, either," he interrupted.

"I loved him. I loved him so much. How could he treat me like that?"

"I knew he was going to betray you, just like I knew Judas would betray me. I could have stopped you from falling in love with Maurice... but then again, you didn't ask for my help. What level of control over your life are you looking for?

"Touché... I see your point."

"Becky, I know you want to keep Shiloh safe, but do you realize that your desire to help her is rooted in your own pain?"

"What are you talking about?"

"How long have you had that sword in your back?"

"What sword?"

He took her hand and helped her stand up, then gently placed his hand on her shoulder and stepped behind her. He grasped the handle of a sword, then moved it a little. "This one."

"Ouch! What are you doing?"

"If you'd like the pain to go away, I can remove it."

"Is it going to hurt?"

"No. You'll feel better when it's gone."

"Well, then, get rid of it."

With a swift motion, he pulled the sword from the middle of her back. "Be careful around backstabbers." She turned to face him. "How do you feel now?" he asked.

"I feel different. I feel… free." Becky looked down and noticed she was now wearing a long, white dress.

"The sword is gone and so is the pain. That's the first part of the healing process, but there's more. When Shiloh was born, her soul was like a beautiful, handcrafted vase. Because of abuse, her soul was fractured—broken into pieces, like pottery dropped on a concrete floor. You and the girls are the broken pieces. I'd like to make Shiloh whole again. These pieces can be put back together—as if she was never broken. But I can't make Shiloh whole unless each of you agrees to it… you have free will. You're free to remain the way you are, living as a broken part of Shiloh's soul. But… there are other options. You could choose to come and live with me in paradise, or you could help Shiloh be made whole—joining to her core personality, the way you were before she was abused."

"I have a question," Becky said with a look of concern.

"I'll try to answer it."

"If I agree to allow Shiloh to be made whole, does that mean I'll cease to exist?"

"Not at all. You'll always be a part of her. Your experience will be different, but you won't cease to exist."

She looked into a pair of eyes that shimmered with sapphire flames. "You really *do* love her, don't you?"

"I do."

"Let's make Shiloh whole."

"Excellent choice. Before we do, if you're willing, I'd like you to tell the others about your decision."

"Of course." Becky's eyes fluttered. Shiloh came back up and Becky returned to the inner world.

The blue-eyed man took Becky's hand and walked beside her on a dark, wooded path. They approached a moss-covered stone wall stretching out in both directions. Gaps appeared in it here and there, where pieces of stone lay crumbling on the damp ground. They turned to the left and walked until they came to an opening in the wall about twenty feet wide. Remnants of hinges clung to the ends of the wall. Ornate pieces of stone covered with moss lay broken and decaying in the gap. A pitiful trickle of water struggled through the gate as they drew near. The path they walked crisscrossed a small stream that carried dark, foul-smelling water. Some of the creek crossings had crude bridges. In other places, the path disappeared into the water and reappeared on the opposite bank. Before long, they came to a crossroad. Continuing straight, the path became a paved street and soon, a row of drab houses flanked them on both sides.

They continued walking until they came to the center of town. The street ended at a black, wrought iron fence that surrounded a small park. In the middle of the park, was a beautiful amphitheater. The blue-eyed man led Becky through a gate, then helped her climb a short flight of stairs to a stage where she stood alone. Becky called the other women and girls, and soon they had gathered around her. Most were toddlers or school-aged, but a few adults came out to hear her. When they had all gathered around, she began speaking.

"You all know how much I love Shiloh. You know how I've fought beside you to try to protect her. Today, for the first time,

I was given a taste of freedom. The anger, pain, and rejection I've lived with are gone. I can't feel them anymore. I feel only peace. That peace came through this man who is called 'Jesus.'" She pointed to the blue-eyed man who stood behind them. "Some of you have heard about or met him."

She wiped her eyes and continued. "After he healed me, he asked if I would be willing to let Shiloh be made whole. He says we can become one, the way we were before she was abused. I won't lie. I'm a little scared. I've heard it said that I could lose myself, if I allow it. But he healed me. And that proves that he loves me. So, I'm going to trust him. I'm asking you all to think about letting him heal you, too. The peace you'll feel is indescribable. Thank you for listening."

Becky walked down the stairs and into the crowd. The girls parted as she passed by. A girl about five years old joined her. Becky took her hand. Several toddlers followed them to the middle of the park where the blue-eyed man waited for them. Shiloh stood next to him.

"If you're ready," he said to Becky, "I'd like you to face Shiloh."

Becky walked toward Shiloh, then stood facing her. "Shiloh, I'd like you to give Becky a hug."

Shiloh gave Becky a tender embrace and then she disappeared. "Thank you, Becky," she said, softly.

The blue-eyed man spoke with each girl and asked them the same question. After they had answered, he gave each of the older girls an embrace and they vanished. He picked up the two toddlers, one in each arm, and they disappeared.

40

Drumar walked between rows of cars in a lot surrounded by a barbed wire fence. The vehicles had missing tires, smashed fenders, and broken windows. Near the entrance to the salvage yard, a machine loaded freshly crushed cubes of painted metal onto a flatbed truck that would soon be on their way to a smelting furnace. Drumar stopped in front of the burned out, twisted chassis of a 1933 Duesenberg. Its once-supple leather seats turned to ash, its legendary engine seized with rust, its gleaming hood ornament removed long ago, by a thief. "Ah, how the mighty have fallen," Drumar said to Bogren, who had just arrived and was standing behind him.

"Good morning, sir."

"I have your latest report on Miss Martinez. Our enemy seems determined to destroy all of your hard work. I had high hopes, Bogren, but I must admit, I'm disappointed."

"I am, too, sir. Her newfound faith is a real challenge. And Charity's work on healing her alters isn't helping."

"All true, my friend. And you've just identified the main problems you're facing. Faith and healing are two things our enemy loves to use against us. But we have something that will work in our favor."

"And what's that, sir?"

"Time."

"I'm not sure I understand."

Drumar pointed to the Duesenberg. "The law of entropy tells us that all great things will eventually fall into decay, given enough time."

Bogren smiled. "And so will Shiloh?"

"She's making strides, but she won't immediately be healed of her emotional wounds. As much as it's a time-consuming process to inflict emotional trauma, reversing it is likewise, a long and arduous process. Time is on our side, Bogren. You can still wreak some havoc in her inner world. There's still time to destroy her hopes. You might consider what damage can be done to her gates, as well. Particularly her faith gate, since destroying her faith is a key to bringing her back to our side."

"I understand, sir."

"You must attack this foolish optimism of hers. I'd like to suggest a time-tested method, if I may."

"Of course, sir."

"Shiloh will naturally have expectations of what church life ought to be like. She'll expect unconditional love, but she'll find indifference. She'll expect to make new friends, but her congregation will be too busy to spend time with her. She'll want counseling, but the leaders will only want to control her. Perhaps one will try to seduce her. Shiloh is going to have wants and needs and most of them will go unanswered. In much the same way that we are experiencing disappointment over her progress, she must be made to feel the same disappointment over her church experiences. Her expectations must never be fulfilled. Disappointment is our best ally, Bogren. And how do we create disappointment?"

"By creating expectation."

"Correct. You must make sure she has high expectations so that she can suffer crushing disappointments. And what do we do when someone suffers one disappointment after another?"

"Exploit them for all they're worth."

"Precisely."

41

Dark clouds swirled in the heavens, drenching the woods in a chilly rain. Leaves scurried through the sky like flocks of birds riding on frenzied winds. A wandering bolt of lightning struck a long-forgotten gate, knocking a silver crossbar into the mud. In a musty, underground dungeon beneath the woods, three dark beings tortured a little girl who lay helpless, secured by chains at her hands and feet.

A party of dark spirits gathered on a path between the village and the silver gate, led by two creatures standing more than thirty feet tall. The ground trembled as they passed. Little ones ran to get out of their way. The party moved swiftly toward the gate.

When they had arrived there, a giant searched the woods until he found a rotten log. The behemoth dragged the log to the edge of the woods and tossed it crosswise into the river. He returned to the woods and when he'd found another one, he dragged it out of the woods and tossed it into the river, near the first one. He went into the woods again and found a third log and tossed it in and continued until he had created a dam. When he was finished, the river had been rerouted. It now flowed away from the gate.

The other giant found a large, dead tree branch and swung it at the gate, bending the main support bar. He raised the branch and brought it down with all his might. The blow bent the silver frame driving one section of it into the ground. He continued his assault until there was nothing left but bent and broken pieces of metal embedded in the mud that covered the forest floor.

Miles upstream, a golden being descended from a dark sky. It passed over the river and circled back, landing near the base of a waterfall. The being had six wings, three pairs on each side of its body. As soon as it landed, it went to the edge of the woods and found a small girl who had been beaten unconscious. The glimmering being applied a bit of oil to her face. A second being descended over the river, and then a third, both landing near the waterfall. As soon as their feet touched the ground, they walked toward the woods, looking for injured girls.

42

"Thanks for coming over, Tina," Shiloh said as she ground a handful of espresso beans and tamped them in the porta-filter.

"Don't mention it, sis. It's nice spending time with one of my favorite people."

"Is two shots enough?"

"That'll be fine."

Shiloh steamed the milk, then tossed in the shots of espresso and stirred the coffee before bringing two cups to the table. She sat down and slid one across to Tina. A worried look appeared on Shiloh's face.

"What's wrong, hon?"

"Everything," Shiloh replied before taking a sip. "This church thing isn't what I'd hoped it would be. I'm going to this church and getting to know some of the people. They seemed nice at first, but no one seems interested in getting to know me. It seems they only have time for themselves. They're either too busy or too disinterested to give me the time of day. I thought I'd make at least a couple of new friends, but it's not happening."

Tina took a sip of coffee. "Look, Shiloh, I've been to a few churches like that. But each church is different. Sometimes you have to do a little looking before you find the one that's right for you."

"This isn't the first church I've tried. Before this, I went to a different one down the road. I started getting to know the pastor and his staff. A woman on the staff kept asking me over and over to sign up to work in the nursery on Sundays. Another man on staff wanted me to be on the fundraising committee for the new addition to the church building. I told him I wouldn't be a good fit for that, but I was interested in being on the prayer team. He shook his head and told me I would have to serve in the church for years before I could be considered for the prayer team. When I told him I'd already seen people healed, he laughed and said that was nonsense—God doesn't do those kinds of miracles anymore."

"You must have been disappointed."

"It's worse. I signed up for a home Bible study group that met once a week, and was getting to know the couple that hosts it. They seemed like nice people, so I confided in them, privately, about my past. But I found out later that when I wasn't around, they were gossiping about me. Apparently, everyone was talking about me—and in the worst possible way. I felt like such a fool for trusting them."

"Oh, Lord—"

"At this point, Tina, I can't try another church. The church is just a bunch of hypocrites—a tank full of smiling sharks waiting to attack. I appreciate everything you and Charity have done. But if this is what church is like, I really don't want anything to do with it. Who needs these fake people and their religion?"

43

Shiloh pulled the blanket up around her face. She let out a sigh and closed her eyes. Although her mind was filled with thoughts of betrayal, she was exhausted and drifted off to sleep.

Standing once again in The Crystal Sea, she reached below the surface and picked up a handful of gemstones. The old man looked at her. "Are you hungry?"

Shiloh hadn't noticed feeling hungry, but suddenly she wanted to eat. "I am," she said.

"Me too." He held out his hand, and she took hold of it. They walked to the edge of the sea, then up a grassy path toward the coliseum. A breeze carried the unmistakable aroma of freshly baked bread. As they walked toward the coliseum, the scent intensified. Arriving at a large door, the old man paused and asked a question. "What would you like for lunch?"

"I like Italian." She looked around trying to see where the aroma of bread might be coming from. "But I don't see a restaurant nearby."

The old man stretched out his arm, and the door swung open.

They walked down the crystal corridor which ended in a vast stretch of the heavens, dotted with planets, stars, and a row of doorways suspended in space. Shiloh looked at them. "What are they?"

"Well," the old man said, "they're doors."

"I actually knew that," Shiloh said with a glance.

"I'm sorry. Of course you did," he replied with a smile. "These doors lead to many different places. Would you like to try one and see where it leads?"

"I'd love to."

"Pick one."

She examined them for a moment. "I want to try that one," she said pointing to the door in the middle.

They lifted off from the ground and drifted toward the door in the center of the row. As they approached, it opened, and they passed through.

They materialized on a street corner. A lush hillside of grass and wildflowers sloped down toward a crescent-shaped bay dotted with private beaches. Sailboats passed in the distance, diamonds danced on the water beneath the setting sun. Behind them, a violin played. They turned to see where the music was coming from. Across the street, was a stone building filled with people, music and food.

"Where are we?" Shiloh asked.

"Palermo."

"Palermo, Italy?"

"I sure hope so," he said with a wink. He took her hand and led her across the cobblestone street. He opened the restaurant door, and they went inside. They followed the waiter to a cozy table near the back of the restaurant where they were seated. The waiter spoke to the old man in Italian. The old man whispered in the waiter's ear. He smiled with approval and left. A few minutes later, the waiter returned with a basket of fresh bread and a plate of seasoned olive oil. The old man tore off a chunk and dipped it in the oil. He lifted it to his mouth and savored it. Shiloh ripped off a large piece and did the same. She looked into the old man's eyes. "I love a lot of things about you, but the thing I miss most is your eyes."

"How are things going since you got back?" She looked down. Words escaped her, but the expression on her face spoke volumes. Tears rolled off her cheeks. "That bad?" he asked.

She avoided looking at him and instead, stared at a man sitting at a nearby table. "Seems like one disappointment after another," she replied.

"Feel like telling me about it?"

"Not really."

"That's a shame. Because I just ordered a lot of food, and we're going to be here for a while."

She looked into his eyes. "Somehow, you always know the right thing to say."

"So, what's got you down?"

"The train wreck of a church I got involved with."

"I see," he said, tearing another chunk of bread from the loaf and dipping it in oil. "Think there'll be any survivors?"

"It's not looking good for the sheep, and it's sure sucking the life out of me."

"Why are you going there?"

"Isn't that what Christians do? Go to church. Pray. Pay tithes. Get screwed over?"

"Did I ask you to do that?"

"Well, no. But I thought that's what I was supposed to do."

"And who told you that?"

"I don't know. It's just the way it's always been."

"Tell me something. You've met a few church pastors, haven't you? Do you like the way they teach?"

"Not really." Shiloh said, ripping off a chunk of bread and dipping it in oil. "How can you teach all those people at once? How can you answer their questions?"

"If you could pick anyone in the world to teach you about me and my son, who would you choose?"

"That's easy. I'd pick Charity," she said, taking a bite of bread.

"She'd be my pick, too. In fact, she's the one I chose to teach you."

"Charity?"

"There's no one you know who understands me better. She's a good teacher. And," he continued, "unlike some people that you're going to run into, she'd never do anything to hurt you."

"Like the people I've already met?"

"The world is full of broken and messed up people, Shiloh. The church is no exception. When the sheep turn on you, and people you think you can trust betray you, it's best to forgive them and move on."

The waiter brought them an appetizer. The afternoon sun fell slowly into the sea.

44

Shiloh walked through the woods. A layer of high cirrus clouds refracted small rainbows in the morning light; sun dogs hovered to the north and south of the rising sun. The filtered light revealed broken lengths of wire and twisted pieces of metal scattered on the forest floor. Stepping around them, she brushed off dirt and debris from the bent crossbar of the gate and rested her arms on it.

Beyond the gate, Anabelle ran as fast as her tiny legs would carry her. Tears streamed from swollen, red eyes. Two dark figures pursued. One jumped on her, tackling her to the ground. She clawed at its eyes. The second fastened a pair of metal shackles to her wrists which were attached to a long chain. The creature hoisted the chain over its back, then dragged her down the path toward a castle. Anabelle's screams alerted Jennifer, who was engaged in her own battle with two dark ones.

Jennifer swung and landed a blow to the face of the dark one that was nearest to her, sending it into the thicket. The other one jumped on her back. She twisted and turned, trying to free herself, but the demon would not let go. She ran down the path which ended at the river bank. As she approached, the dark one wrapped its hands around her eyes. Her foot caught the exposed root of a tree, which sent them somersaulting toward the water. Jennifer stretched out her hands to brace for the fall. The demon let out a scream of terror. The instant they hit the water, the body of the dark one exploded. Jennifer dove deeply, swimming several yards from the riverbank and surfaced only to find pieces of the creature's body floating all around her.

She swam toward shore, carefully maneuvering between the dismembered body parts, which emitted a putrid odor. She pulled herself from the water and looked around to get her bearings. Staring at her from the thicket was the other dark one. Knowing she'd just found a way to destroy her tormentors, boldness rose up in her. "Unless you want to end up like your friend, you'd better leave us alone." The creature held its ground. She took a quick step toward the dark one. It turned, let out a screech, and fled deeper into the forest.

A shining one circled in the sky, then dipped lower and passed a few yards over her head, landing on the riverbank. Its golden body glowed like a lantern. Six wings, three on each side of its body, flapped slowly in the breeze. She stepped closer until it was within arm's reach. The being looked at her. "Are you hurt?"

"No, I'm fine. The darks, however, didn't fare as well."

The shining one turned and began gathering pieces of the shredded demon that lie along the riverbank. A second one with three pairs of wings appeared overhead. It glided to the riverbank and waded into the river to retrieve pieces of the corpse. As she watched, a third being glinted in the sunlight above the river. This one was larger than the others and had two pairs of wings. It passed overhead, then circled back, landing just a few yards away.

She stepped closer. "Excuse me… but I've never seen a shining one with four wings."

The glimmering being stepped closer, "The shining ones *you* know are healers. They're here because those who live here need healing. They also keep the realm clean. But things have changed. You've discovered the power that the water has over the dark ones. And now you must destroy them with it. I'm the Captain of the Lord's army. I'm here to help you defeat them."

"Defeat them? We're used to being attacked by them. You want *us* to attack *them*?"

"May I ask your name?"

"It's Jennifer, but the littles call me Jen."

"What is your responsibility to Shiloh?"

She looked at the ground. "I protect the littles, but we have no weapons. The littles are terrified and the screaming never ends."

"It sounds to me as if you could use some help."

She hesitated and then nodded.

"You discovered that the water is deadly to the dark ones. If you use your imagination, I'm sure you'll find ways to weaponize it. The darks know that you've discovered the power of the water. That will frighten them. They'll soon realize they must attack you. If they don't, it's only a matter of time before you destroy them. They have no choice but to attack. They'll try to put you and the others at a disadvantage. The best strategy is to take the battle to them before they attack you."

"So, we need to figure out how to use the water as a weapon to destroy them?"

"That's part of the plan. But there are other weapons I can give you. Are you familiar with the shining one called 'Jesus?'"

"I am," she replied.

"What do you think of him?"

"He's amazing. I cry every time I think about how he died to set me free."

"Would you like to receive his weapons of warfare?"

"I would love that."

The shining one gently placed his hands on her head. "I give you the helmet of salvation." A barely visible, silvery helmet appeared around her head. He touched her shoulders. "And the breastplate of righteousness." A protective layer formed around her torso. "And the sword of the spirit." A long, silver sword appeared in her hand. "And the boots of the good news of the kingdom." A pair of rugged hiking boots materialized on her feet. "And lastly, the shield of faith." In his hand, he held a smooth, large, golden shield. "Perhaps I should explain this one. It operates according to your faith. When you have faith, it's quite useful. When you're fearful, it's of no use." He held it out. "Would you like to try it?"

She took hold of the shield. Immediately, it shrunk to a size no bigger than her hand. She blushed with embarrassment. "It takes a little practice." He placed his hand on her shoulder. "Close your eyes. Now imagine a dark one coming toward you from the woods." He took hold of her hand that held the shield. "I'm with you," he whispered in her ear. "Now I want you to see us attacking the dark one with the sword. She raised the sword and swung it. "Now open your eyes."

She looked at the shield which was now the same size that it had been when he handed it to her. "Faith?" she asked.

"Faith, trust, confidence. Call it what you will. When you trust that the shield will protect you, it will."

"I understand."

"You're going to need more than weapons and water. I'll send more shining ones to bring food. You can find it by the waterfall.

I'll also arm any believers. Are there others besides you?"

"Yes."

"Have them meet me at the waterfall."

"I'll let them know."

"In fact," he said, "it may be better to have them come down to the waterfall and live there for a while—especially the littles. As long as there are dark ones around, you'll all be safest near the river."

Shiloh smiled. She bent down and pulled a twisted strand of silver wire from the dirt. She stepped away from the gate and navigated her way through the broken pieces, then tossed the wire on the ground. She turned again and closed her eyes. In her mind, she saw a delicate but regal gate made of welded and woven pieces of gleaming, new silver. She stretched out her hands. "Rise from the mud, and be made new. Let the bent and twisted things be made straight. Let the broken places be made whole. Let this gate be restored to its original design." The pieces rose from the ground to form a shining, new, silver gate.

45

An eagle perched atop a large boulder, clutching a snake in its talons. The serpent twisted wildly, struggling to free itself from the grip of the bird. The eagle made a quick strike with its bill, digging deeply into the flesh just behind its head. It pulled away from the snake's body, and the head snapped off like a dandelion severed from its root. "I do admire your spirit, my reptilian friend," Drumar said, "but it's just not your day." A dark form appeared in the ravine below. Bogren quickly made his way up the wash until he stood a few paces away.

Drumar drew a long breath. "Bogren," he said, still looking at the eagle, "I received your latest report on Miss Martinez. I expected more from you. You need to get this situation under control before you lose her forever." He turned to face his pupil.

Bogren trembled slightly. "Things in the inner world have taken a turn for the worse, sir. I'm sorry. I didn't see it coming."

"Is there anything that you *do* see coming, Bogren? Have you any foresight, at all? Any common sense? Or are you completely blind to the patterns of her behavior? How did you not see this coming?"

"I'm sorry, Drumar. I don't quite know what to say. Please forgive me."

"Dammit, Bogren! This isn't about forgiveness. Forgiveness is for fools. This is about victory! And *you* are about to lose! Do you realize what's at stake? You had one opportunity after another to bring her to our side, and you wasted them. You had better start taking your job seriously, or you'll find yourself wallowing in the abyss with the other useless tormentors who fail to capitalize on their victim's weaknesses!"

"I understand, sir."

"If you understand, Bogren, what is your plan? What is your strategy? I'm tired of excuses. I need to hear something from you that will give me confidence that you'll turn things around."

"Yes, sir. I do have a plan."

"Let's hear it, then."

"Shiloh's system has discovered the power of the water. It won't be long before they'll be able to use it against us. As I see it, we must act quickly and decisively with overwhelming force. I would like to request reinforcements to overpower the enemy and completely destroy them before they destroy us."

"I agree with your assessment. We can't waste time. I'll put in the request for reinforcements. As soon as they've arrived in her system, put them to work."

"Of course, sir. Is that all?"

"Yes, Bogren. You're dismissed. Keep me updated on your progress." The demon slipped back into the ravine and drifted back down the hillside toward town.

46

Shiloh rang the bell and waited excitedly for the door to open. She set down a fabric bag that held brushes, paints, and assorted tools. Janet opened the door and gave her a hug, then they disappeared inside.

Shiloh set out her brushes on a small table next to an easel. She secured a rectangular canvas to the easel. In the previous session, she'd blocked in her composition including the trees of a dark forest. In the foreground, a grassy meadow scene needed more detail. She squeezed paint from tubes onto her palette—black, umber, yellow, ultramarine and cerulean. She mixed two colors together with a palette knife.

"Remind me again what this scene is," Janet said.

Shiloh grabbed a brush and loaded it with color. She finessed the paint across the width of the bristles, leaving the excess on the palette. "It's a place I sometimes go with the girls when we want to get away from the dark ones." She stood at arm's length from the canvas, and with the paint on her brush, she drew the shape of a shadowy, almost human figure standing at the edge of the meadow.

"A dark one?"

"Yes." Shiloh squeezed more paint onto her palette, using her palette knife to mixed some lighter, warmer colors for the foreground.

"Shiloh, you should be proud of how your skills have advanced. It's remarkable how much progress you've made. And your confidence has really grown."

Janet prepared a few canvases at a large table. She was always nearby, ready to do an impromptu demonstration when Shiloh asked about how to create a certain effect or how to mix colors. As the day turned to evening, the painting began to reveal the reality of Shiloh's inner world. Four little girls sat in a field of wildflowers beside a clear brook. Their attention focused on a shining, blue-eyed man who sat in their midst, while shadowy beings watched from the woods.

47

Shiloh was on the floor, lying on her side, her knees pulled up to her chest. Charity sat on the floor next to her. They had been through this before and Charity always prayed it would be the last time. "Shiloh, can you hear me?"

"Shiloh not here. Shiloh with littles."

"What's your name, honey?"

"We Jasmine. We scared. Darks coming."

"Jasmine, my name is Charity."

"Are you dark?"

"I'm not a dark, Jasmine. I'm Shiloh's friend."

"We like Shiloh. She loves us."

"I love Shiloh, too. Jasmine, what does the sky look like?"

"We inside. Can't see sky."

"Jasmine, I need you to go outside and look at the sky."

"We scared."

"Don't be scared, Jasmine. I'll help you."

"We open door. We go outside."

"Good, girl, Jasmine. What do you see?"

"Dark sky. Dark clouds. Very dark. Very windy. We scared."

"Don't be scared, Jasmine.

"We hear darks screaming."

"Jasmine, can you see the river?"

"We see it."

"Do you see any shining ones?"

"No shining ones. Only darks. We scared. Darks all around. They hurt littles. Very windy."

"Jasmine, honey, I need you to go to the river."

"We try."

"Good girl."

"It dark, Charity. We scared."

"Don't be scared, Jasmine. I'm with you."

"Okay, Charity. We at river."

"Good girl. Jasmine, do you know where the waterfall is?"

"We know it. Shining ones live there."

"That's right. It's where the shining ones are. Can you find the waterfall?"

"It far away. It dark. It windy. So windy. We scared."

"Don't be scared, Jasmine. If you stay by the river, nothing can hurt you."

"Dark ones close, Charity."

"I want you to walk beside the river to the waterfall. If the dark ones come, go into the river. They can't hurt you in the river."

"Darks getting closer, Charity. Darks scream so loud. We scared."

"Splash water at them."

"We try. We splash dark one. Oh, no! Dark one go boom! Stinky dark!"

"Are there more darks by you?"

"Dark ones run away."

"Good girl, Jasmine! Good girl! Stay by the water, and walk toward the waterfall."

"Getting darker now, Charity. So dark. Can't see."

"Jasmine, I want you to say these words, 'Lord, you're a light on my path. You're a lamp to my feet.'"

"Lord, you light our path. You lamp our feet… oh! It work. More light now. We see better."

"Okay, Jasmine, keep moving toward the waterfall."

"Darks flying, Charity. They scream so loud. We scared."

"They can't hurt you in the river, Jasmine. Keep walking toward the waterfall."

"More darks ahead. They scream. Littles running. Screaming so loud."

"Jasmine, can you get the littles to come to the water?"

"We try."

"Good girl."

"Auntie Jen with us now. She bring littles to river."

"Great. Follow Auntie Jen. If you see dark ones, splash them with water."

"Lots of darks now, Charity. So many. They angry. They screaming. Littles splashing darks. Darks go boom! Smelly darks. Eeew. Stinky darks."

"Keep moving toward the waterfall, Jasmine. Stay by the river.

"It dark again. So dark. Can't see."

"Say it again, Jasmine. Say, 'Lord, you're a light on my path and a lamp to my feet.'"

"Lord, you light our path. You lamp our feet… okay, more light now."

"Good girl, Jasmine."

"We scared. Ground shaking now. Littles splashing darks.

Darks screaming. Darks go boom. Darks go into woods. So loud. We scared."

"You're safe, Jasmine. Stay with Auntie Jen. Can you see the shining ones yet?"

"We see them."

"Keep walking with Auntie Jen. She'll help you get there."

"We at waterfall with shining ones, Charity. Many littles here. Very loud, now. Darks screaming. Darks flying in sky. So windy. Littles splash darks. Darks go boom!"

"Jasmine, do you see Shiloh?"

"Shiloh here. She talking to shining one."

"Jasmine, ask Shiloh to come up."

"We ask."

Shiloh blinked her eyes, and slowly sat up, looking confused for a moment. "Hey there," Charity said, "busy night with the girls?"

"You wouldn't believe it if I told you."

"No need. Jasmine's been giving me the play-by-play. How's it looking?"

"Never seen so many damn demons in my life. It's like hell emptied itself into my backyard. It's all-out war. And there are hundreds, maybe thousands, of shining ones—sorry—angels. The defenders are armored up, taking out the dark ones. The littles are hanging out by the waterfall with an army of angels, splashing and blowing them up whenever they come near."

"Sounds like the good guys... I mean, the good girls, have things under control. How do you feel?"

"Killer headache, but I'll get over it."

"Coffee might help."

"That would be wonderful."

48

A generation ago, downtown Gilbert was a watering hole for farmers and ranchers. To this day, hitching posts are still found outside many of the storefronts. Romeo's is a romantic cafe tucked away behind some shops on the main drag. Sitting at a table in the corner of the restaurant, Ken looked at the menu. "So many choices. Can you recommend anything?" He ripped off a piece of bread from a loaf that sat in a basket, dipped it in seasoned olive oil, and took a bite.

"I don't see Spam and rice on the menu, but they do have a killer bacon-wrapped pork tenderloin," Shiloh said.

"Well, that's disappointing. I really had my heart set on Spam and rice." He laughed. "What looks good to you?"

She leaned over and kissed him. "You're looking pretty good to me, sailor."

He kissed her back. "Babe, that waiter is going to come back. And if we don't decide on something, he might throw us out."

She kissed him one more time, then picked up the menu and

220 · PRAYING MEDIC

flipped through it, "I'm torn between the Transylvania chicken and the coconut fried shrimp. The chicken sounds delicious, but I'm afraid it might bite back."

"Don't worry, my beloved. Ken, the vampire slayer, will keep you safe from those bloodsuckers."

"Did you just call me your 'beloved?'" Her eyes grew wide. He leaned over and kissed her again.

The waiter came to the table. "Are you ready to order?"

"We are," Ken said, sitting up straight.

Shiloh glanced once more at the menu. "I'll have the Transylvania chicken and a glass of your house Merlot."

"Excellent choice, madam." He turned to Ken. "And you?"

"Since you're all out of Spam and rice, it looks like I'll have to settle for the bacon-wrapped pork tenderloin."

The waiter smiled. "You won't be disappointed. Anything to drink?"

"Iced tea with lemon would be fine."

"I'll get that started for you right away."

"Shiloh, I've been meaning to ask how you're doing as far as space goes for your painting business?"

"It's getting pretty cramped at Janet's place. With both of us working there, we're running out of room."

"Have you looked into getting your own studio?"

"I have. Prices for commercial space are out of my budget right now. If I could count on selling three or four originals a month, I could probably swing it, but if I don't sell, it would put me in a financial bind."

"We have some commercial space that I don't think anyone is using. Let me talk to my family. We may be able to make some room for you. How much space do you think you'd need?"

"A thousand square feet would be plenty."

The waiter returned and placed their drinks on the table. Shiloh took a sip from her glass. "Who would have thought a couple of years ago I'd be looking for my own studio space?"

"I don't know what your future holds," Ken said, "but I do know one thing. When you follow God's plans, things can get a little crazy. And you better hang on because it's gonna be a wild ride."

49

Shiloh crawled into bed and brought the blanket up around her shoulders. She reached to turn the lamp off. "Okay, Dad, if you have a dream for me, I could really use it tonight." She closed her eyes, and in a few minutes she had drifted off to sleep.

She stood once again in the coliseum. The blue-eyed man stood beside her. They looked at the door in front of them. Are you ready?" he asked.

"Let's do this."

He stretched out his left arm, and the door opened. He kept his right arm behind his back as they moved into the corridor, then he suddenly stopped. "Wait. This occasion is a bit more formal." He brought his right arm out from behind his back and held out a full-length, crimson-red dress. "Do you like it?"

"I love it!"

"Close your eyes," he said. "Now open them."

When she opened her eyes again, she was wearing the dress. He looked at her from head to toe and raised one eyebrow. "It's definitely you. And now we're ready to continue." He took her hand, and they walked to the edge of coliseum, which seemed to have no ceiling or walls and no floor. They beheld a luminous expanse of planets, stars, galaxies, and nebulae, suspended by nothing. Her mouth hung open as she looked at the blue-eyed man. "Go ahead," he said. "Take a walk among the stars."

She moved among the galaxies like a giant in a city of ants. She passed through the celestial scene without disturbing so much as an asteroid. The planets and suns passed right through her. It was as if she were seeing the cosmos from the perspective of God. After inspecting the larger stars and a few nebulae, she took her place at his side again and slipped her hand comfortably into his.

"It's… it's…" she struggled to find words.

"I feel the same way sometimes." He smiled at her. "Let me show you one more thing." He waved his hand, and the scene began shrinking, until it was no more than the width of his hand—still hanging in mid-air, but now, surrounded by darkness.

"There are more dimensions in the heavens that you can imagine, Shiloh. Tens of thousands more realms than you've ever dreamed of." He turned toward the stars and said, "Let there be… more light."

In an instant, another expanse of stars appeared before them, but, this time, the light given off by them had a distinctly golden hue, which dominated the other colors. The first group of stars was still visible, but the new ones dwarfed them.

Shiloh turned toward him again. His sapphire eyes had become a fiery mix of orange and amber. The faint, blue flames that she occasionally saw became a raging fire. His hair was no longer brown, but white. He gazed into her eyes.

"Shiloh, when you first arrived here, you had very little light. But your light has become brighter through the things you've experienced. We refer to that light as our 'glory.' All the light that you see in the entire creation is the glory of my father and me. And as you go through life and grow in wisdom and knowledge, you're being changed by the glory you behold. You're being shaped, little by little into a closer reflection of me. That's the purpose for which you were created. One day you will look in the mirror, and you will no longer see the Shiloh you were years ago. You'll see a reflection that looks like mine."

He took her hand and turned her around. Before her was a mirror. "What do you see?" he asked. She looked and saw their reflection as they held hands.

"I see you and me."

"Now look at me."

She looked into his eyes of fire. "Now, look again in the mirror." She looked once more and saw him as a brilliant, luminous spirit that emanated rays of light of every color. Next to his reflection was hers—an almost exact image, with the same luminous spiritual body but wearing a crimson dress. "This is the woman you are becoming. You and I are one. And you are my beloved." A wave of love pierced her heart.

"I love being your beloved," she whispered softly. "It's all I've ever wanted. You seem like a man who knows how to be faithful to his woman and true to his word."

"Faithful and true?" he said with a smile. "I like the sound of that. Maybe I'll have it tattooed on my leg." He took her hand and led her through the celestial scene back to the hallway where they'd entered.

50

Shiloh sat on the warm, smooth rock, looking over the valley. Far below, cars traced the path along Highway 60 eastward from Phoenix toward Mesa and then on to Apache Junction. The wind coming up out of the valley blew wisps of coal-black hair away from her face.

"Are you ready?" Charity asked.

"I think so," Shiloh said, looking over the valley.

"Take a look inside, and tell me what you see."

Shiloh closed her eyes. She flew through the woods, soaring above the path until she neared a stone gate. The broken parts of the wall that she'd seen before were no longer scattered throughout the woods. The wall was continuous, and the moss which had covered much of it was now gone. The beautiful, ornate shapes that had been formed in the stone gate appeared as new. A clear stream of water flowed from under the finely crafted doors toward the woods.

"The western gate, I don't even recognize it. It's completely different. The wall has been repaired, and the gate looks like new. And there's a river flowing out of it. The water is crystal clear."

"Perfect," Charity said. "How does the weather look?"

"Mostly sunny with a few clouds."

"Great. Now let's find a blue-eyed man."

Shiloh walked the path alongside the stream. A lone, dark-winged being circled above her. She followed the small stream to an even larger one, and a waterfall came into view from above. Standing at the base of the falls, waist deep in water, was a blue-eyed man who shone like the sun. As she drew closer, dark beings fled into the woods. She stood beside him in the river. "I found him."

"Okay," Charity said, "now we need to know if he's the real one. Does he have wounds in his hands?"

Shiloh took his hands in hers and noticed a wound in each one. "He's got wounds in his hands."

"Ask how he got them."

"Where did these wounds come from?"

"They were put there for you," the man said.

"He said they were put there for me."

"That's him," Charity said. "Ask him if he'll go with you."

"Will you follow me?"

"That's usually my line," he said with a wry smile, "but yes, I'll follow you."

"Okay, Charity, he said he'll follow me."

"Alright, I want you to go straight to the amphitheater and call the others."

"Charity says we need to go to the amphitheater."

"Lead the way."

Shiloh waded to the bank of the river with the blue-eyed man following behind her. As they emerged, she grabbed his hand

and began walking briskly toward the path that led toward the village. "Come on. We need to find the others." Shiloh led the blue-eyed man down the road that led into town, past the houses and then to the park surrounding the amphitheater.

Out of the corner of her eye, she saw a butterfly coming near her. She stopped and placed her hands on the wrought iron fence that ringed the park. The iridescent, blue-winged creature came closer and closer until it landed, gently, on her nose. "Yesterday he was a worm," the blue-eyed man said. "But because he was willing to go through the necessary changes, today, he's something completely different.

Shiloh stood motionless staring at the butterfly, its wings moving slowly, back and forth. When it had flown away, she passed through the gate and climbed the stairs to the stage, then called to the women and girls, "I need to speak to you all. It's very important." Out of the homes came the women and children. The tall and the small. The timid and the brave. When they had all gathered around, and only after she had made eye contact with each one, she addressed them.

"Thank you all for coming. We've been through an incredible battle, and I want to thank you all for protecting me. I want each of you to know that I love you. An important day has arrived. A day that gives us an opportunity to change, not for the worse, but for the better. Becky and some of the others decided they wanted to be healed. Although you no longer see them, they haven't ceased to exist. They're still a part of me, just like you're a part of me. And they're happy. They're free. A few of the girls chose to go with Jesus to be with him and they're living in the most incredible place. Now, it's your turn. Jesus is here, and he's willing to heal you. He'll take away your pain, your shame, your anger, and your fear. But only if you're ready."

A tall woman named Patricia stepped from the crowd and made her way up the stairs and onto the stage. "Listen, everyone. At first, when I thought about being healed, I was afraid because I didn't know what would happen to me. But after the battle we just went through, I know Jesus and I know he would never hurt me. I'm tired of the battles with the dark ones. I'm sick of seeing the littles hurt by them. And I'm done fighting with you all over control. I don't know about the rest of you, but I'm ready to be healed." She descended the stairs and walked to the back of the crowd where the blue-eyed man stood. She looked into his eyes. "I'm tired."

"What do you do for Shiloh?" he asked.

"I protect her from her father."

"Shiloh's father can't hurt her anymore. She's safe now."

"Sometimes I feel like he's still here... waiting for a chance to hurt her again."

"Do you feel angry?"

"Sometimes I want to kill him."

"If you did kill him, you'd be just another killer. Is that what you want for Shiloh?"

"No, of course not."

"I'd like to heal the pain you're feeling, Patricia. But first, why don't we deal with that anger?"

"What do I need to do?"

"Repeat after me. I release my anger. I forgive Shiloh's father. And I ask him to forgive me."

"Wait. Why do I need to ask for *his* forgiveness? He's the one who hurt me."

"Patricia, he was wrong. But wanting to kill him is just as wrong. This isn't about him. It's about you. Your anger isn't helping Shiloh."

She took a deep breath. "I release my anger. I forgive him, and I ask for him to forgive me."

"That wasn't so hard, was it?" He placed his hand on a festering wound on her shoulder. "Be healed." He reached inside his robe and pulled out a pair of wire cutters. A barely perceptible ring of metal had encircled her head. He snipped it, and it fell to the ground. "How do you feel now?"

"It's strange… all I feel is peace." Patricia looked at herself and saw she was now wearing a white robe.

"A little forgiveness goes a long way.

"How about the memories?" she asked. "I can't stand them."

"Would you like to give them to me?"

"How do I do that?"

He held out his hands, and a silver box appeared. "This is a memory box. Any memories you don't want, you can put inside it."

"There are some memories I'd like to get rid of forever."

"Here's what I want you to do. Look inside yourself and find the memories."

Patricia closed her eyes and examined her memory bank. She sobbed. "I have them."

"Okay, grab hold of them, and place them in the box." She reached into the depths of her being, and pulled them out one by one, and placed them in the box.

"Patricia, would you like to become one with Shiloh now?"

"I would."

He motioned for Shiloh to stand in front of him, then he had Patricia face her. "I want you to step into Shiloh as if you were stepping into a waterfall." Patricia stepped toward Shiloh and then disappeared.

"Thank you, Patricia," Shiloh said, softly.

The blue-eyed man turned toward the women and girls who were looking on, "Who wants to be next?" A girl about six years old stepped forward. "What's your name?" he asked.

"Jasmine."

"Where do you hurt?"

"She pointed to her belly."

He knelt down and asked, "Can I touch your tummy?"

"You not hurt me?"

"I promise I won't hurt you."

"Okay, you touch me."

He gently placed his hand on her, and suddenly a yellow butterfly flew out from beneath her shirt. And then a purple one. And then a green one. They continued coming out faster and faster, each one a different color, until a small tornado of butterflies enveloped her. She ran around the park, giggling. Slowly, the butterflies dissipated. When they were gone, she came back to him. "How do you feel now?" he asked.

"Like a butterfly!" she said, still giggling.

"Would you like to become one with Shiloh?"

"Like Patricia?"

"Yes, like that."

She shrugged her shoulders. "Okay."

"Can Shiloh give you a hug?"

"Yes! We love Shiloh!"

He turned to Shiloh. "I'd like you to hug her."

Shiloh knelt down and looked into Jasmine's eyes. She wrapped her arms around the girl and she disappeared. The blue-eyed man turned again toward the crowd. "Who's next?" A teenage girl stepped forward. "What's your name?"

"Demon."

"That's an unusual name. Can I ask how you got it?"

"It's what everyone has called me, as long as I can remember."

"When was the first time?"

"Shiloh was at church with her aunt and I was up while the preacher was talking. When he was done, he said if anyone needed prayer, they should raise their hand. I raised mine and pretty soon a bunch of people gathered around me. Someone said I wasn't Shiloh because that's not how she talked. Someone else said I was a demon. The next thing I remember, four or five people grabbed hold of me and told me to come out. 'Get out of her, Demon! Get out of her right now, in the name of Jesus, you filthy demon!' They tackled me and more people grabbed me and screamed for me to come out. 'Get out of her, you evil Demon! Get out of her right now!'"

"Do you like the name Demon?"

"Not really."

"Is there a name that you like better?"

"I've always liked Abigail."

"That's a nice name. Do you know what it means?"

"No."

"It means 'the Father's joy.' You may not have brought much joy to your earthly father, but your Dad in heaven thinks you're the bomb. So, from now on, your name is Abigail."

"Good morning, Abigail, would you like some tea? Yes, I would, thank you. No problem at all, Miss Abigail." She smiled. "Oh, I like it. I like it a lot. Much better than Demon."

"What's your responsibility, Abigail?"

"To protect Shiloh from religious fanatics who don't understand her... or us. But now she has you. I hurt so much. I just want the pain to go away."

"Abigail, turn around." She turned to face the other way. Before her was a curtain of water twenty feet high that splashed onto a sandy patch of ground. The water didn't come tumbling over a cliff. It seemed to come out of nowhere.

"It's beautiful."

"Step into it."

She walked toward the waterfall, but before stepping in, she stopped and turned to look at the blue-eyed man. He looked at Shiloh. "Why don't you join her?" Shiloh walked toward Abigail, then took her hand. They stepped into the waterfall together.

Abigail pointed her head upward with her eyes closed. The cascading water hit her in the face, full force. "Thank you for protecting me," Shiloh said.

Abigail looked down, allowing the water to run off her head onto the ground. "The pain is leaving."

"You're so brave."

Abigail flung her hair over her head and looked at Shiloh. "It's gone. The pain is gone! I feel so good."

Shiloh looked at the blue-eyed man. He gave her a nod. "Are you ready?" she asked.

Abigail looked into her eyes. "I am."

Shiloh held her close until she disappeared. The girls looked on. Shiloh stepped out of the waterfall. "Who's next?"

One by one, the girls came forward. The blue-eyed man asked about their responsibilities. Then he asked them to give him any painful memories, and then, he healed them. After they were healed, he merged them with Shiloh. When there were only a few women left, he turned to Roxanne. "How about you?"

"I'll pass. Shiloh still needs me to protect her."

"I understand. The tide has definitely turned. The dark ones are on the run, but there are still plenty to be dealt with. I can give the defenders better weapons and armor, but only if they're willing to follow me."

"I've been thinking about that. Seems like some of what I was told about you may have been wrong. I'm not ready to trust you just yet. But if I change my mind, I'll let you know."

"You know where to find me."

51

Shiloh steamed the milk, then pulled a shot of espresso, and then another. She added each one to the cup, then two pumps of chocolate syrup, a bit of cream, and topped it off with a delicate swirl. She carried it to the counter and sang, "Here's your mocha, Louie."

A short man in a yellow t-shirt, blue shorts, and red suspenders took the drink from her hand. His eyes squinted at her through thick lenses and dark-framed glasses. "Thanks, Shiloh." He took a sip. "Perfect," he added before dropping a dollar in the tip jar and taking his usual seat under the foliage of a potted palm tree near the front door.

A tall woman in an iridescent, peacock-blue dress moved to the counter. Oblivious to Shiloh, she studied the paintings that hung on the wall behind the counter.

"How may I help you, ma'am?"

There was no response. The woman's gaze was locked on a square painting featuring blue and green rays of light coming from what appeared to be a gate. Shiloh shot Charity a puzzled glance. "Excuse me, ma'am, is there something I can make for you?" Shiloh asked.

Tearing her attention away from the painting, the woman replied, "You don't happen to know the artist, do you?"

"The artist?" Shiloh looked in the direction where the woman had been staring. "Well, actually… I'm the artist."

"You did those?

"Yes."

"All of them?"

"Yes, all of them."

"May I ask your name?"

"It's Shiloh… Shiloh Martinez."

The woman grasped her hand and shook it slowly. "Camille Carrington. So nice to meet you, Shiloh."

A young man in a black hoodie, black straight-leg jeans, and flip-flops looked up from his phone with an annoyed expression. "If she's not going to order anything, can I get a hot, medium, soy latte, to go? I'm in a hurry."

"Oh, of course. I apologize. Please, take care of your customers, Shiloh, and… is there any way I might have a closer look at your work?"

Charity came over. "Hi, I'm Charity McBride, the manager. If you'd like to take a closer look at Shiloh's paintings, she'll be happy to show them to you." Charity looked in her friend's eyes. "I'll take over." She confirmed that the young man wanted a soy latte.

"Can you make it a triple-shot?"

"I sure will. Sorry to keep you waiting. It's on the house." The woman standing behind him looked at her. "Okay, okay," Charity laughed. "Your drink is on the house, too."

Shiloh led Camille behind the counter where four paintings hung on the wall. Shiloh removed one and handed it to Camille who began inspecting it. She turned it around to examine the back and then the edges. "I'm impressed."

"Thank you. Do you have any questions?"

"I have many questions. But first I should tell you who I am. I'm the owner and manager of the Carrington Art Gallery in Scottsdale. I'm always looking for new talent. Are you represented by an agent or a gallery?"

"Not right now."

"Have you ever considered having one represent you?"

"I've spoken with Janet about galleries a little. Oh, sorry, Janet is a friend… and mentor. She taught me most of what I know about painting."

"Has she?"

"Oh, yes. She's pretty amazing."

"May I ask what Janet's last name is?"

"Sinclair."

"You're a student of Janet Sinclair?"

"Yes. Do you know her?"

"Everyone in the Scottsdale art scene knows Janet. And they adore her. I didn't know she was teaching again." She hung up the first painting and began inspecting the others.

"She's been helping me—teaching me. She's become like a mother to me."

"Well, you are a blessed woman."

"Yes, I am."

Camille looked at Shiloh expectantly. "Do you have other paintings besides these?"

"I have about twenty-five or twenty-six plus these four. So around thirty, altogether."

"Are you showing your work anywhere else?"

"Not yet, but I hope to in the future."

"Shiloh, I'd like to see the other paintings. If they're like these, I'd like to discuss having the gallery represent you, if that's something you'd be interested in. How are your Saturdays?"

Shiloh blinked. *A gallery owner? From Scottsdale?* "I'm usually at Janet's studio on Saturdays, so that would work for me."

"May I come over this Saturday, say, ten a.m.?" She pulled out a business card and handed it to Shiloh.

"Let me check with Janet and I'll let you know later today."

"Perfect."

"Can I get you a drink before you go?"

"I'd love an Americano."

"I'll have it ready for you in a couple of minutes."

Camille smiled and took a seat. In a daze, Shiloh prepared the drink and brought it to the table. "This one's on me."

52

Shiloh sat in a chair in the living room. Charity sat on the couch. "You've come a long way, sis," Charity said. "I hardly remember the old Shiloh."

"If it weren't for you, I'd still be a mess. I feel completely different. So many wounds have been healed on the inside. She looked at the scars on her arms and rubbed them. Tears welled up in her eyes. "My show is next weekend, and everything is perfect... except for one thing. I've prayed and I've prayed and I still have these stupid scars."

"Did you ever think to ask me?"

Shiloh looked away, "You've done so much already. I couldn't ask you to do anything else. And what if you prayed and nothing happened?"

"So, you're not even going to give me a chance?"

Shiloh looked at Charity, "Do you think you can make them go away?"

"Won't hurt to try." Charity got off the couch and sat on the floor in front of Shiloh, then placed her hands on her scarred forearms. "Skin, I command you to be healed, right now. I release the healing power of the kingdom of God. I command all soft tissue to be healed, restored, and made brand-new. Scar tissue, I command you to leave."

Shiloh looked at her arms in disappointment. "That's what I was afraid of. No change."

"You know healing isn't always immediate. Give it some time."

53

Paintings were displayed with care along the outside walls of the Carrington Gallery. Shiloh glanced at them with pride, in a full-length, crimson-red, sleeveless dress. Camille and Shiloh smiled, welcoming visitors as they entered. A young man on Camille's staff directed them to review the artist's statement displayed near the first painting.

Ken and Charity stood in the corner of the room talking with Tina and the other employees from Mocha's. "I can't believe Shiloh is having her own art show!" Tina said.

"And who would have thought she'd wear a sleeveless dress?" Charity added.

Tina looked at Charity with a grateful smile. "Thank you for believing in her and praying for her. Everyone should have a friend like you."

Shiloh's eyes met Charity's, and she came over to join the group. "Thank you all for coming to the show."

"We wouldn't miss it for the world," Tom said.

Tina touched Shiloh's left arm gently. "A miracle."

Shiloh rubbed her left hand along her right forearm—not a scar or a needle mark. "God has been so good to me." Shiloh looked at Charity. "How can I ever thank you?"

Charity smiled, "Sell some paintings. We'll call it even."

Ken gave Shiloh a hug. "You look like something out of a dream," he said, smiling proudly.

"You don't look so bad yourself," she said with a grin.

Guests meandered from painting to painting, wine glasses in hand. Camille worked the crowd, making small talk with new guests, and laughing with familiar patrons. Sometimes together, and sometimes separately, Camille and Shiloh answered questions as they were summoned to one painting or another.

A portly man with silver hair and a beard said, "Shiloh, your work is fascinating. Am I to understand that the inspiration for this painting is some kind of 'inner world' in your soul?"

"Thank you so much, and yes, that's correct. I'm sure you've read my statement. The inner world is where my personalities live. Adult personalities are sometimes called 'alters.' Child alters—at least in *my* inner world—are called 'littles.' Many psychologists believe that the inner world is imaginary. But it's as real to us as the physical world is to you.

"Can you tell me more about this particular painting?"

"Sure. This piece shows one of the gates at the entrance to my inner world. You'll notice the dark clouds and stormy weather. The weather conditions of the inner world reflect the moods—the peace or turmoil—going on in the soul. And do you see the dark, shadowy figures hiding in the trees? These are what we call 'dark ones.' Spirits that torment the parts of our soul."

As Shiloh spoke, she noticed Camille walking toward her with a middle-aged couple. They moved closer to listen to her description of the inner world. Camille gave Shiloh a nod of approval, then addressed the silver-haired man, "May I interrupt for a moment? I believe Mr. Pierce has a question that may interest you as well."

"Certainly. Go right ahead," said the silver-haired man.

"Yes, thank you. Miss Martinez, I came here to meet you tonight because I have a personal interest in this topic. Would you say that dissociation and the inner world are strictly caused by major trauma, or is there more to it?"

"Thank you for coming. It's nice to meet you. You've asked a good question. Based on what I've learned, it doesn't have to be *major* trauma. Everyone suffers some level of emotional trauma in life, right? It's hard to avoid. If the trauma experienced is *minor*, it can cause slight dissociation but it doesn't create well-defined, separate personalities."

Mr. Pierce nodded in agreement. "That's what I thought. So dissociation happens any time the main personality isn't in full control, but perhaps at a lower level on a spectrum?"

"Right," Shiloh said. "A person who experiences minor trauma may not be aware of an inner world. But a person who experiences severe trauma through ritual abuse, for example—where distinct personalities are formed—is usually aware of their inner world."

Camille found a tall, young woman with a question and brought her into the conversation. "Shiloh, you seem to be remarkably well-functioning for someone who's suffered such severe abuse. How have you managed to do all this?"

"It's a very long story. But it involved two people who loved me unconditionally throughout the process. The first is my best friend, Charity. She's the lady standing over there with long blonde hair. She walked me through the process of healing and loved me even when I was unlovable. The other person is Jesus.

If it weren't for him, I wouldn't be alive right now."

Through the evening, Camille's staff helped the patrons make their purchases, reminding them that the paintings would be shipped or delivered after the last day of the exhibit. Shiloh continued answering questions and talking with guests. At nine-thirty, Camille thanked the guests for coming and announced that the gallery would be closing in thirty minutes. She reminded buyers to make their final purchases at the front table.

Shiloh returned to the corner where her friends were gathered. They greeted her with approving smiles. "I feel bad for ignoring you all night," she told them.

"Don't worry, hon," Tina said. "This is your night, and we're glad to be here to celebrate it with you. We're so proud of you!"

Charity addressed the group, "I'd like a few minutes alone with Shiloh." The two walked to a corner of the gallery, and spoke quietly. "I hate to be the materialistic one—but I'm dying to know—how many paintings did you sell?"

"Hang on a minute. Let me find out." Shiloh walked over to Camille, whispered in her ear, and Camille whispered back. She returned to Charity, and in a hushed voice, said, "I sold more than half the paintings!"

"Wow, that's fantastic!"

Suddenly, Shiloh heard a thought that wasn't hers. *I have big plans for you. Wait and see.*

"You've come so far," Charity said, "and I know Dad has big plans for you."

Shiloh gasped and looked at Charity with wide eyes, "That's *exactly* what Dad just said."

54

The sun hovered over the Superstition Mountains, turning the layer of early morning clouds into a blanket of pink cotton candy. Shiloh stopped to take pictures. When she was finished, she stowed her camera in her backpack and took Ken's hand. They continued hiking. South Mountain Park is the largest County Park in the nation, spanning twenty thousand acres, most of it covered with hiking trails. Non-human residents include lizards, jackrabbits, coyotes, roadrunners, and quail. Most of the plants will draw blood if you get too close to them, including agave, saguaro, prickly pear, and Teddy-bear cholla. Except during brief monsoons, the rivers are dry year-round—their banks covered with mesquite, creosote and palo verde trees.

"I miss the islands," Ken said, "but the sunrise over the valley is worth getting up for."

"The islands. Seems like your destiny is waiting there for you," Shiloh said, pensively.

"The islands are indeed calling. I can see staying in Phoenix maybe another year or two, but there are a lot of unfinished plans waiting for me in Hawaii."

A couple of hikers passed them on the left. "I've been thinking about that," Shiloh replied." Your friend's business is there and he's not moving to Phoenix. I don't have family here. I can paint just about anywhere. My life is pretty mobile—except for Charity."

"I know how close you two are. And I would hate to see you separated."

"I've come a long way since I first met her. She's an amazing friend and great teacher. But every student has to step out from the shadow of their master and make their own way." The trail steepened. Shiloh breathed harder.

"Are you seriously considering leaving Arizona?"

"I'm weighing my options."

"Hawaii isn't just where my next job is located. Mom is there, and she needs help. After all you've been through, you just might be the person who can help her."

"I always thought of myself as the victim. Never the helper. But I've learned to see myself differently. And you're right. With all I've learned, maybe I can help your mom."

"What about Charity?" Ken asked.

"I'm sure I'd miss her like crazy. But we have phones and video chat. I don't think it would be hard to stay in touch."

"I never thought it would be this easy talking to you about moving to Hawaii."

"A year ago, I wouldn't have considered it. But now, I see it as just another curve in the road—another adventure with God."

55

Shiloh stood beside the gate. Its doors of finely crafted gold hung wide open. She stepped into the clear running stream that coursed through its opening. She wiggled her toes, letting them dig into the sandy bottom. She took a deep breath, then exhaled and began walking against the flow. Soon, she was knee-deep in the river. She followed it about one hundred yards north, then stepped out onto the river bank, and followed a well-worn path upward toward a rocky overlook. The peaceful, blue sky framed by junipers and yellow pine filled her with peace. She ascended the trail to the highest point and then continued walking along the rim of the canyon until a prominent outcropping of rocks appeared which looked out over the valley. She sat down near the edge and surveyed the canyon below.

Out of the corner of her eye, she caught a shadow moving across the rocky ground. Dread quickly filled her heart. Before she could turn, Bogren's hands were around her throat, and he drove her to the ground. She dug her nails into his face. The demon let out a scream but tightened his grip. She beat against his chest with her fists. Fear overwhelmed her. She wondered how much longer it would be until she became unconscious. The blue-eyed man appeared in her mind. Swimming underwater and then surfacing in her memory. *You mean if I believe I can breathe underwater, I can?*

A spark of hope ignited in her soul and spread throughout her body. Fear dissipated. A confident smile appeared on her face. Bogren laughed. "Keep smiling, fool, you'll be dead in a minute."

She wedged her knee between her body and the demon, and extended her leg just enough to cause his grip to loosen and her voice to be heard. "I speak into existence a deep pool of water." She wrapped her arms around the demon and wrestled him until they rolled over the edge of the cliff. As they fell, she shoved the demon away from her and then oriented herself to land in the water, feet first. A still, deep pool materialized just before her feet broke the surface. She plunged into the water. Bogren's body disintegrated on impact, flinging pieces in all directions. Shiloh came to the surface and looked around. She swam downstream until she came to a sandy bar just above a waterfall. A shining one descended from the sky and landed on the water, then quickly began removing pieces of the demon's body from the river.

Shiloh followed a familiar trail that led to the bottom of the waterfall. There, on a large, flat rock, beside the river, sat the blue-eyed man. She walked over and sat down beside him and slipped her hand into his. He looked back into her eyes—eyes that danced and flickered with their own fiery brilliance.

ABOUT THE AUTHOR

Praying Medic (Dave Hayes) is a podcaster, public speaker, and author. He's written hundreds of articles and numerous books—both fiction and non-fiction. Prior to his career as an author, he worked as a paramedic for 35 years.

INKITY PRESS™

Other books from Praying Medic
For up-to-date titles go to: **PrayingMedic.com**

Series—The Kingdom of God Made Simple:
Divine Healing Made Simple
Seeing in the Spirit Made Simple
Hearing God's Voice Made Simple
Traveling in the Spirit Made Simple

Series—My Craziest Adventures with God:
My Craziest Adventures with God - Volume 1
My Craziest Adventures with God - Volume 2

Series—The Courts of Heaven:
Defeating Your Adversary in the Court of Heaven
Operating in the Court of Angels

And more:
Emotional Healing in 3 Easy Steps
God Speaks: Perspectives on Hearing God's Voice (28 authors)
A Kingdom View of Economic Collapse (eBook only)
American Sniper: Lessons in Spiritual Warfare (eBook only)

SCAN THIS TO GO TO
PrayingMedic.com